Clint drew Tyra in, his blood pounding through his veins. "A passionate woman should never have to go two years without being kissed."

"I'm thirty-five years old. I've surveyed the field, and the good guys are all taken."

Sliding an arm around her waist, he tucked her in close. Ah, she felt good. "Did you just insult me?"

"Except you, but I can't have you."

"Not on a regular basis, but you can have one kiss to tide you over."

She nestled against him and rested her palms against his chest. "Not a good idea." But judging from the glow in her eyes, the rest of her was in favor of that plan.

"No one ever has to know."

Her breath hitched. And her lips parted.

"I can keep a secret if you can." He slowly lowered his head.

ROPING THE COWBOY'S HEART

ROWDY RANCH

Vicki Lewis Thompson

Ocean Dance Press

ROPING THE COWBOY'S HEART
© 2023 Vicki Lewis Thompson

ISBN: 978-1-63803-939-6

Ocean Dance Press LLC
PO Box 69901
Oro Valley, AZ 85737

Visit the author's website at
VickiLewisThompson.com

Want more cowboys? Check out these other titles by
Vicki Lewis Thompson

1

"Hey, there, daaarlin. Will yooouu be myyy Vaaalintiiine?" Clint McLintock flipped a switch and listened to the playful buffalo moan he'd just recorded. Real buffalos didn't sound anything like that. But the large wooden mascot who stood inside the entrance to the Fluffy Buffalo sounded exactly like that. Spoke English, too.

The identity of the guy who'd first created that voice years ago was a well-guarded secret. From the first day Clint had hired on at the Buffalo he'd tried every which way to worm the story out of the owner, Frank Lindquist. No dice.

Then one night Frank had come out of the office and discovered Clint entertaining customers at the bar by mimicking the buffalo's speech. After closing time, Frank had offered him a raise if he'd polish his delivery. They needed recordings made in preparation for updating the electronics.

Oh, really? Had the previous guy died? Retired? Since Frank had been close-mouthed in the past, Clint hadn't bothered to ask.

He'd accepted the challenge though, convinced it would be easy. Nope. He'd auditioned for Frank many times before getting the green light.

He'd begun recording at Frank's house in a spare room converted to a soundproof recording studio. From the lived-in feel of the studio, he guessed the unknown previous guy had used it. Frank had sworn on a stack of Bibles it wasn't him.

Clint believed that. The bar owner didn't have the pipes to achieve a deep, mournful tone. These days Clint still recorded in Frank's spare room, except Frank was in Arizona with his second wife. He'd turned the house and the bar over to his only child, Tyra. Clint's high school crush.

He'd been a lowly freshman. She'd been the most popular girl in the senior class, a glowing presence greatly missed at Wagon Train High when she'd left town for law school. After Clint graduated, he'd waited tables at the Buffalo, which included the added benefit of working alongside Tyra during her summer breaks from school. He'd created plenty of fantasies about that redhead. But now that she was his boss, he'd locked them down for good. Keeping the job he loved depended on it.

The overhead light flicked on and off, a signal that Tyra wanted in. The switch had been relocated outside the door to serve in place of a knock, which could ruin a recording.

"All clear!" Taking off the headphones, he pushed back the desk chair and went to open the door.

Tyra wasn't dressed to impress. Her favorite extra-large sweatshirt hung almost to the knees of her faded jeans. Her fuzzy slippers had seen better days. She hadn't put on makeup, either, so her face looked exactly as nature had intended. Without mascara and eyebrow pencil, her lashes and brows were lighter, giving her a softer, more vulnerable look.

She could glam it up with the best of them, so her lack of effort verified their close, but strictly platonic, relationship. She held two open bottles of cider dangled from the fingers of one hand and a bowl of fragrant popcorn in the other.

He smiled. "Aren't you a welcome sight."

"Thought you could use a break and a snack." She sashayed in. The woman had rhythm, a factor in making her the best head cheerleader Wagon Train High ever had or likely would have.

"Great timing." He relieved her of the popcorn and cider. "I have three versions. Need you to pick one. Or tell me to start over." He set the popcorn and drinks on a side table. Gesturing toward the desk chair, he pulled over a stool for himself.

She settled in and picked up the headset, but instead of putting it on, she looped it around her neck. "You sure have a warm tush, McLintock." A lock of flame-colored hair escaped the haphazard arrangement she had going on. She tucked it behind her ear.

"Warm tush, cold heart."

"Then I guess it wasn't you who took your little brother's shift so he could go to a Carrie Underwood concert last week."

"Had to. Can't stand to see Rance cry." If she wanted to chat a bit before listening to the recordings, she was the boss. And she fascinated him. Always had, ever since the first pep rally of his freshman year.

The chasm between them had been huge then. It had narrowed slightly when they'd been co-workers for a couple of summers. Then she'd finished her law degree and accepted a job in D.C. working for a non-profit.

This outcome, with Tyra assuming ownership of the Buffalo right after Frank had made him the manager, was straight out of the movies. And here they were on a Monday night, taking advantage of her day off and a slow evening at the Buffalo to finalize a Valentine recording they wanted in place by eleven in the morning. The big day was only a week from tomorrow.

"Did you do anything fun today?"

"I finally had lunch with Rachel."

He frowned. "Who's—"

"From the cheer squad."

"Oh, right. The little one you guys used to put at the top of the pyramid."

"Would you believe she has four kids and her oldest is a teenager already?"

"Yes, ma'am. Most of the guys I graduated with are married with kids. I'm the exception."

"Me, too, when it comes to that."

"You and Rachel must have had a lot to catch up on."

"We did, but then the conversation sort of dragged. I blame myself. I did a lousy job of keeping up with friends from high school and I'm learning it's nearly impossible to come back after all these years and pick up where you left off. People change."

"They do."

"Anyway, enough of that. Let's hear what you've got."

"Sure thing." Leaning over, he cued up his first version. "Each one has a slightly different emphasis." This close she smelled way better than the popcorn. More like chocolate chip cookies. "Have you been baking?"

"Cookies."

"Then why'd you bring popcorn?"

"Goes better with cider. You can have cookies later, if you want some, after we finalize this."

He laughed. "Keeping the talent happy?"

"That's my goal."

Turned out their goals were aligned. He wanted to make her happy, too. That inspired some totally inappropriate thoughts that could get him fired if he said them out loud. "I hope *the talent* has come up with something that works." He scooped up another handful of popcorn.

"I'm sure you did. I can't believe I erased the old one, but it gives us a chance to improve on the original. You can't just toss out *Be my Valentine* and be done with it. You have to put emotion into it."

"Maybe, but when it comes from a wooden buffalo—"

"Don't overthink it. The buffalo is a stand-in for whoever the customer hopes will say those words. It might even jumpstart their dinner partner to say them."

He smiled. "You're a true romantic."

"And you aren't?"

"No comment." If he didn't know better, he'd say she was flirting.

"Which tells me you absolutely are. And like most men I've known, especially the cowboy variety, you'd rather die than admit you're hard as nails on the outside and soft and squishy on the inside."

"The first version of the buffalo sounds soft and squishy on the inside."

"Aww, because he's lovesick."

"Or he has indigestion. Hard to tell the difference between those two."

"No, it's not." She put on the headset, pushed Play and grinned. Pausing the recording, she slid the earphones down and glanced at him. "He sounds like some poor guy whose invitation to prom was rejected by the only girl he wants."

Clint shuddered. "Every teenage boy's nightmare."

"I doubt you were ever turned down."

"No, thank God. But then I had to go through it again when I impersonated Cheyenne."

"You got him a prom date? And the girl didn't notice it was you?"

"No, because the staging had to be so dramatic. What used to be a simple question asked between classes had become an elaborate production."

"The promposal. Dad told me the craze hit Wagon Train after I'd left. Must have been stressful, especially for the guys."

"Not so much for me, but Cheyenne hated the concept and begged me to handle it for him."

"Just like when you took his place at the bachelor auction last year?"

"Yes, and for the record, I was against doing the auction thing for him. I tried to tell him those days were gone, that our looks had become more distinctive and folks would figure it out. I tried coaching him, but he's...."

"Not a born performer like you." Her green eyes glinted with amusement and something else... awareness?

"I wouldn't say I'm a born—"

"Come on, Clint. It takes one to know one. I was angling for that head cheerleader position from the first time my folks took me to a game. I loved every minute of being on the squad."

"Probably why you were so great at it."

Her cheeks turned pink. "You remember when I was—"

"Vividly." Whoops. That sounded a wee bit too enthusiastic. He shrugged. "I was a hormonal teenager."

"Cute, though. You made an impression."

His blood pumped faster. Stupid. "You're thinking of Cheyenne. He's way better looking."

"Your twin is handsome, but you have Chris Hemsworth eyes. And you put yourself out there. I remember you as a freshman. You had promise."

Oh, great. Now he was blushing. "We should probably get on with this. The cider's getting warm."

She gazed at him. "You're discombobulated."

"No, I—"

"I think you had a crush on me in high school."

He avoided her too-knowing gaze. "Who didn't?"

"Oh, plenty of guys, I assure you. They told me I was stuck up and full of myself."

"Which proves they were idiots."

"I know that, now, but back then those comments hurt. I didn't realize I intimidated them."

"Like I said, knuckleheads."

She smiled. "Unevolved. It's been years since I dealt with that, and yet it still feels great to have you call them out after the fact."

"Then I'm glad I did." He'd always put her on a pedestal. Evidently other guys had tried to knock her down. If he'd known, he would have taken matters into his own hands. Likely would have been outgunned and taken a beating, but it would have been worth it.

"It's lovely to interact with a guy whose ego isn't threatened by a strong woman with a brain."

"Thank you, but full disclosure, at fourteen I wasn't focused on your brain."

She smiled.

"But now I am. Totally focused on your brain."

"You're a terrible liar, McLintock." She held his gaze for one electric moment. Then she looked away and cleared her throat. "We need to finish this thing."

"Yes, ma'am." His heart raced. Whether she'd meant to or not, she'd just telegraphed sexual interest.

But now her movements were brisk and businesslike as she put on the headset and started the next recording.

Meanwhile he struggled to get his bearings. She was attracted to him. That was good news and bad news. He wouldn't make a move. That would be suicide. What if she did, though?

2

Tyra knew better than to flirt with her manager. She was a lawyer, for God's sake. Never mind that Clint would never sue her for sexual harassment. Six months ago her *warm tush* comment would have been part of the silly banter they'd fallen into. Tonight, not so much. She had to be more careful, way more careful, or she'd put them both in an impossible situation.

During her first year as owner of the Buffalo she'd been too busy learning the ropes to pay much attention to her capable manager. She'd been grateful for his excellent advice, friendship and sense of humor. But over this second year, as she'd gradually adjusted to the routine, Clint's hotness had been impossible to ignore.

He was thirty-one to her thirty-five, but that didn't have the significance it used to. Their age difference wasn't a problem. Their boss-employee relationship, though... big problem. She'd seen businesses go down the tubes when personal entanglements mucked up the works.

Time to settle the heck down. She listened to the next two recordings, took off the headset and pushed the chair back. That left them free to sip cider and eat popcorn without endangering the equipment. She kept the conversation on track while they discussed the choices.

When they agreed to use candidate number three, she gave her seat to Clint so he could finalize the process.

He finished off his cider before reclaiming the chair. "That's my favorite version, too. Sincere, but not deadly serious."

"Exactly." She took the stool he'd vacated. He'd warmed the wooden seat, too. She didn't comment on it. "He sounds like you."

"Let's hope not. Do you think that will come through?"

"Not to anyone else, because nobody thinks it's you. It does to me because I know it is."

"I've worried about that. My family's speculated on it for years. Some think it was your dad. Now that he's moved away—"

"It wasn't him."

"Do *you* know who it was?"

She shook her head. "He never let me meet him. I heard them murmuring downstairs when he'd arrive, but I wasn't allowed to come down. I think Mom knew, but she wouldn't tell me, either."

"Very strange."

"All I know is he quit doing it and now you're the replacement."

"I'm glad Frank picked me. It's fun. I'd do it for nothing."

"Then I'll adjust your salary."

"I misspoke. If the Buffalo couldn't afford me—"

"Kidding!" She waved toward the desk. "Please do what you need to do."

He grinned. "Yes, ma'am."

While he concentrated on his work, she admired how his shoulder and arm muscles moved under the soft cotton of his Western shirt. He had great hands, nimble fingers. What would they feel like if he—

Stop it, dummy! She took a last gulp of cider and glanced away. Was he more enticing than usual? Or had her attraction reached the boiling point? Either way, she needed to get out of this room sooner rather than later.

"Done." He took off the headset and flashed her a grin. "Do I get cookies, now?"

"Right! You certainly do." She picked up the empty bottles and stood. "Be right back." She hurried down the hall, loaded several cookies on a plate and set off again, moving fast. She couldn't easily kiss a guy who was eating cookies.

Wait, *kissing*? Was she seriously in danger of doing that? She skidded to a stop and the cookies almost landed on the floor. She nudged them back to safety.

Before she charged back into the tempting scenario, she needed a game plan, a sensible approach. How about getting this inconvenient attraction out in the open? Talking about it might lessen its power.

Armed with her strategy, she walked into the makeshift recording studio. "As promised." A good hostess would ask if he wanted coffee with the cookies. But that would extend his stay. She wouldn't suggest coffee.

"Those cookies look and smell delicious."

"Thanks." She moved the popcorn bowl to make room for the plate of cookies.

"Some might say that fresh popcorn, cold cider and homemade chocolate chip cookies constitute a meal."

"Those people wouldn't have a healthy diet." She glanced at the popcorn bowl. She'd nibbled on it but hadn't eaten much. Yet the bowl was empty. "I'll make a wild guess you didn't eat dinner before you came here."

He shrugged. "I knew this had to get done so I just came over." He picked up a cookie.

"Then you only get one." She snatched up the plate as he reached for a second.

"Hey." He laughed. "We had a deal, lady. I held up my end. Cookies, please."

"Come into the kitchen." She shoved her misgivings aside. His good health was important to their business, after all. "I'll warm up some vegetable soup. You need to eat something nutritious before diving into the cookies."

He stood, amusement flickering in his blue eyes. "I realize you're my boss, but I'm pretty sure this is the first time you've ordered me around."

That stopped her. "You're right. Sorry. I suddenly morphed into my mother. That's embarrassing."

"I thought it was funny."

She took a breath. "Would you, um, like some homemade veggie soup? Feel free to say no."

"If I say no, will I get cookies anyway?"

She rolled her eyes. "Yes, you will. I'll put some in a bag to take with you. But when you get home, I hope you'll eat something before you—"

"Just teasing, boss. Couldn't resist. Homemade veggie soup sounds wonderful. Thank you for offering."

"Then come on back." She walked down the hall and into the roomy kitchen. "My mother insisted on regular meals and wouldn't pass out the treats until I'd finished a reasonable amount of food that was good for me." She took the pot of soup out of the refrigerator, set it on the stove and switched on the heat.

"My mom's the same. She's always after us to—" He paused. "Well, you know."

She glanced over her shoulder. "It's fine for you to talk about your mom." Turning back to the soup, she lifted the lid and dipped the ladle in to stir the contents. "Do I envy you because she's alive and mine isn't? Yes, I do. I'm working on being happy for those who have a mom instead of feeling envious, so it's good for you to give me practice." She replaced the lid and faced him.

The caring in his expression took her breath away. Shoving both hands in her pockets, she battled the urge to reach for him and soak up all that warmth and compassion.

"Life's not always fair." He took a step closer, as if he might haul her into his arms. Then he swallowed and backed away, thrusting his hands in his pockets, too. "I can't imagine a world without my mom in it, and yet you've been experiencing that for... how long?"

"Eight years, although sometimes it feels like she died yesterday. I almost dropped out of law school. She was my biggest supporter, the one who encouraged me to go for it, and we'd hatched all kinds of plans for a celebration when I passed the bar."

"But you didn't quit."

"Dad said she'd want me to finish, and of course he was right. And then I got the exact job I wanted. She would have been thrilled about that."

"The D.C. gig was your dream job?"

"Sure was." She turned back to the stove and lifted the lid. Steam drifted up, warming her face. "Soup's ready."

"What can I do?"

Obviously his mom had taught him well. "There are bowls in the cupboard to your right and spoons in the silverware drawer right below it."

"I'm on it." He opened the cupboard. "Are you having some?"

"Um...yes." She'd meant to eat after he left, but that seemed silly now that she'd invited him back here.

He got out two bowls and two spoons. "You haven't eaten, either?"

"No, and before you ask, I wasn't planning to eat those cookies I brought out." She filled each bowl as he handed it to her. "They were for you. I somehow assumed you'd had dinner at the Buffalo before you showed up here."

"No, ma'am. I was intent on getting this project finished."

"Well, thank you for being so dedicated." She left the burner on low in case he wanted seconds and surveyed the table where both bowls sat catty-corner from each other on a bare surface, the spoons already in the bowls. The setup was efficient but lacked charm. "We need to do this right."

"What do you mean?"

"We need placemats, napkins, and two more bottles of cider. And crackers. If you'll take the cider out of the fridge, I'll get the crackers and the other stuff."

"Okay."

While he twisted off the tops to the bottles, she fetched two quilted placemats, a couple of matching cloth napkins, and dumped crackers into a basket. "That's better."

"Your mom would approve?"

"Yes." She gestured toward the table. "It's official. I'm turning into my mother."

"Nothing wrong with that." He pulled out one of the chairs and gestured for her to sit. "I didn't know her well, but I know my mom liked her a lot."

"And vice-versa. My mom thought a lot of yours." She took her place and then he took his.

Putting his napkin in his lap, he glanced at her. "I've always wondered why you left D.C. to take over the Buffalo, especially if you loved your job."

"When Dad announced he was selling so he and my stepmother could move to Arizona, I was shocked. It was as much a part of my childhood as this house."

He nodded. "I get that, but that job of yours was—"

"Seemingly perfect. Providing legal support to a wildlife organization suits me. But living in D.C. isn't my style. I'm a wide-open-spaces girl." She dug into her soup so he'd start eating.

After his first mouthful, he caught her eye. "Tastes amazing. Thanks for sharing."

"Anytime." Uh-oh. Did she mean that? Had she just issued an invitation to join her for dinner whenever he felt like it? Maybe so. And it sounded like a wonderful idea.

She sucked at drawing boundaries.

3

Anytime? Had Tyra just signaled that she'd welcome him at her table on a regular basis? Probably not. People often said things that they didn't mean.

Except she didn't. So he'd take it at face value. "That's a nice offer. I promise not to abuse it."

"I know you won't, Clint." She reached for a cracker. "You're not the type."

"Thanks for that." The soup really was terrific and he was hungrier than he realized. He had to pace himself and not wolf it down.

Conversation helped. "I understand coming home so you could keep the Buffalo in the family. I understand not loving the big city. But you worked damn hard for that law degree."

"That's why I've become licensed in Montana."

"You did? When?"

"Just recently. Had to take a few courses and pass the bar exam here."

"You really have been busy."

"That's my middle name."

"Gonna hang up your shingle over the Buffalo's front door?"

"Not quite. But I will put the word out that I'll work pro bono for any wildlife organizations in the state who need me."

"That's generous."

"I can afford it since I have a solid income from the Buffalo."

"I know you're a whiz at time management, but still, you'd essentially have two demanding jobs."

She beamed at him. "Yes, but I also have you. Dad told me you'd make my job easy, and you have."

The compliment caught him unawares and heat rose from his collar. "Thank you."

"No, thank *you*. You work hard and with great efficiency. You never complain and you regularly make me laugh. I couldn't ask for a better manager."

"I love my job."

"It shows." The light in her green eyes intensified. "You're an amazing guy."

He tensed. She was leading up to something. "And?"

"I need to level with you."

"Okay."

"I like you."

"I like you, too." Continuing to stare into those incredible eyes was asking for trouble. But he couldn't look away.

Instead, she was the one who broke eye contact. "I'm also attracted to you."

He swallowed. "I picked up on that."

"When?"

"Tonight. And I'm honored."

"That's sweet of you to say, but being attracted to you is problematic. Once I agreed to come back and take over, I gave myself a crash course in business management. A boss/employee relationship, especially in a small business like this, can wreck—"

"Say no more. Just tell me what—"

"Can you make yourself less sexy?"

Huh? "How can I—"

"Exactly! It's who you are. You're charming, you're funny and you're hot. The women all love you and the guys admire you. Even if you could tone it down, it would be bad for business."

"But—"

"Please don't change anything. I just wanted to get it out in the open in case I'm ever abrupt or distant with you. It's my problem and I'll—"

"It's our problem."

She blinked. "Our problem?"

"I had a crush on you in high school and I've never quite gotten over it. If I had a job over at Miller's Hardware, I'd have asked you out by now. Chances are you've sensed that, just like I can tell you're interested in me."

"I refused to let myself think about it."

"But the chemistry's there and we're both dealing with it."

"Yes. And I don't want to lose my most valuable employee by putting the moves on him. So I won't. You have my word on that."

An emotion flashed in his eyes? Disappointment? His jaw tightened. "Then we're agreed." His soup bowl was empty and so was his cider bottle. "I should be going."

"You haven't had any cookies."

"If you'd be willing to put a few in a bag, I'll eat them on the way home."

"Be glad to. I always forget about your long drive to Rowdy Ranch. What if I added an efficiency apartment to the Buffalo? There could be enough room out back if—"

"Thank you for the thought, but I'm fond of my house. Never had a desire to live in town."

"But you work in town."

"And Rowdy Ranch is home. My cabin was built to my specs. I'm five minutes away from the barn where KoKo is stabled, so I can take a ride whenever—"

"Your horse?"

"Yes, ma'am. Do you ride?"

"I know the basics. If the horse is steady I doubt I'd fall off."

He smiled. "Doesn't sound like you're chafing at the bit to get on one, though."

"At the moment, with all I have going on at the—"

"Then I won't bother asking you to come out to the ranch sometime for a ride."

"In the middle of winter?"

"Sure, unless there's a heavy snow. A week from tomorrow my whole family will go for a morning ride, weather permitting."

"Don't forget a week from tomorrow is Valentine's Day."

"'It's also my little sister Angie's birthday. She knows I'll be working that night, but I promised to be on the ride in the morning and stay for lunch. I've already arranged for midday backup since Rance won't be available, either."

"Do you take a morning ride on everyone's birthday? If you do, I don't remember—"

"Just Angie's. That's her special thing. We do other stuff for the rest of us."

"I'd like to give you both the whole day off, but with the crowd we expect that night, I—"

"Not a problem. When Angie was younger, it was different, but she's turning twenty-five. She can handle having some of us duck out now and then." He pushed back his chair. "Thank you for feeding me. The soup was great."

"I'll get you some cookies." While he carried their dishes to the sink, she quickly loaded cookies in a bag and handed it to him. "Thanks for making this recording a priority."

"The Buffalo is definitely a priority. My family sits at the top of the list, but the Buffalo is in the number two spot."

"I can see that. Thank you, Clint."

"You're welcome, ma'am." He looked around. "Left my jacket and hat in the studio."

"Oh. I'll—"

"No need to see me out." He met her gaze. "I'll come in at 10:30 tomorrow to set up the recording. Sleep well."

"Thanks." She hugged herself to contain the shiver of longing his warm glance inspired. "You, too."

4

Tyra opened the back door of the Buffalo at eight-thirty the next morning, bags of decorations hooked over each shoulder. She was eager to start. When she'd agreed to take over the business from her dad, she hadn't factored in this perk.

She'd missed the thrill of transforming a large space, adding color and lights to produce an exuberant mood. In high school she'd earned a reputation for her ability to. turn the gym into a wonderland. She'd volunteered for the committee as a freshman and soon was put in charge of homecoming, the Christmas formal, and the prom.

A non-profit struggling to raise funds for wildlife conservation wasn't the appropriate venue for elaborate holiday decorations. She'd dialed back her expectations while working in D.C. The Buffalo gave her permission to indulge herself. A festive atmosphere was good for business.

Last year she'd ordered red napkins to go with the white tablecloths they already owned. She'd added red and white carnation bouquets to each table, a heart-shaped wreath of carnations on the door and a crown of carnations for the buffalo.

Mindful of her budget, she'd bought some large shiny hearts to hang from the ceiling and called it good.

This year she was going for great. By shopping sales soon after Valentine's Day last year, she scored enough garlands to cover the rustic walls with hundreds of red hearts. Red heart-shaped lights would surround the bar's antique mirror and the bandstand.

A heart-shaped chrysanthemum wreath on the front door would be illuminated with fairy lights and so would the buffalo's flowered crown. The shiny red hearts from last year would still hang from the ceiling, but she'd spent Monday morning covering them with glitter.

Setting the bags on the floor, she walked into the storeroom to fetch their tallest stepladder. If she worked fast, she might get everything up before eleven.

As she hauled the stepladder out of the storeroom, she came face-to-face with Clint, freshly shaven and gorgeous. Her heart rate picked up. "What are you doing here two hours early?"

"Good morning to you, too."

"Sorry." She gave him a quick smile. "I just didn't expect you."

"On the way out last night I saw all those bags sitting in your living room. I figured you'd come in early like you sometimes do and decorate by yourself, but there were a lot of bags, so I came to help just in case you hadn't asked a server to be here."

"That's very generous." And contradictory. The fizz of attraction had already hit her system and nobody else was due to arrive until at least ten. After their conversation the night before, why was he deliberately creating a time they'd be alone in the—

"I asked Rance to help, too. He should be here any minute."

"Oh!"

"Just following best practices." He gave her a crooked smile.

"Thank you." The fizzy bubbles all popped. And she was relieved about that. Right?

"I like to think we could handle putting up a few decorations, but I—"

"Howdy, howdy, howdy!" Rance barreled in and closed the back door with a bang. "It's freezing out there! Not much warmer in this place! Did you guys turn up the heat?"

"I did not." Tyra couldn't resist. She grinned at Clint. "Did you?"

"No, and I don't intend to." He winked at her.

"I saw that wink." Rance shoved back his hat. "Why the heck keep the heat down?"

"Because it's automatic, little brother. It'll switch on all by itself."

"Yeah, but when's that, dude?"

"When the time's right." He slid Tyra a quick glance, eyes twinkling.

She'd started their word play, but he'd been more than willing to keep it going. That was pure Clint, grasping every opportunity to enjoy the moment. With Rance as chaperone, they could afford to joke around. But sadly, the time would never be right to switch on the heat.

"Well, I can see something about this topic is cracking you two up. In any case, I'm leaving my jacket on. And my hat. And scarf. Have to take off my gloves, though. Fortunately my hands are naturally warm. I have excellent circulation. It's my superpower." He surveyed the ladder and the bags. "Where do we start?"

Tyra walked over to a bag and pulled out a box of heart-shaped lights. "I got a bunch of these."

"Hey, cool! Where do they go?"

"Around the mirror behind the bar and on the bandstand."

"I'll do that!" He started toward her. Then he paused. "I mean, unless you'd rather have me work on something else." He looked over at Clint. "I don't want to hog all the good stuff."

"You're welcome to hang the lights." She handed him the bag.

"I'm on it, boss." He carried the lights over to the bar. "We also need some decorating music," he called over his shoulder. "Some Valentine music. Any requests?"

"*The Rest of—*" Tyra stopped speaking because Clint was naming the same album, *The Rest of Our Life* by Tim McGraw and Faith Hill.

Rance laughed. "That's impressive. Did you two discuss this before I got here?"

"We're just psychically attuned," Clint said.

"Then Tim and Faith it is. And coffee. Who's up for a pot of fresh brew?"

"Me. And if you'd add a peppermint stick to mine, I'd be much obliged." Tyra picked up the ladder and carried it to the back wall. "Clint, the garlands are all in the two gray bags, if you could please bring those."

"Yes, ma'am."

She positioned the ladder in the left corner and turned. "I'm impressed that you didn't rush to take the ladder from me."

"Wouldn't dream of it. I've seen you wrestle a taller one than that."

"When?" The scent of coffee drifted from the bar.

"I'm sure you don't remember, but I volunteered to help decorate for the Homecoming dance my freshman year."

"*That's* when I first noticed you! I was trying to picture the setting." The first song poured from the Buffalo's top-of-the-line speakers. She paused to listen before returning her attention to him. "I didn't know you liked this album."

"No reason you should know. We've never talked about our preferences in music."

"Come to think of it, you're right."

"Or our favorite days of the week."

She blinked. "You have favorite days?"

"Doesn't everyone?"

"Maybe." Hers were the evenings he came over to record. That was telling.

"We also haven't discussed soft-bristle toothbrushes versus hard-bristle."

"Now you're being silly."

"My point is, we've concentrated on talk about work."

"Until last night."

He nodded. "And look where it got us. Sticking to work topics is our safest bet."

"I can see that, but now that we've opened the subject of music, would you be willing to tell me which track from this album is your favorite?"

"This one." He paused. "You?"

"Same."

His blue gaze softened. "Don't know as I've ever told anyone how much I identify with this song. I didn't discover it until after I passed thirty and boy, does it speak to me."

"Same here." She smiled. "Thanks for sharing." And now she'd think of him every time she heard it. She'd be wise to delete it from her playlist. Fat chance.

5

Rance could be a royal pain in the ass, but Clint had never been more grateful for his little brother's presence. The combination of Tim and Faith on the sound system and Tyra's lithe body perched above him on the ladder would have been his undoing if Rance hadn't been around.

One glance up that ladder and the years fell away. He was a lovesick fourteen-year-old gazing at the unattainable woman of his dreams. Time had been gentle with Tyra. She looked much younger than thirty-five, much younger than he did, truth be told.

Could be the result of her indoor lifestyle versus his outdoor one. Whenever he wasn't at the Buffalo or sleeping, he was pitching in on ranch repairs, cleaning out the barn or exercising whichever horses needed it. In the summer, he played baseball with his family if they could gather enough players.

Clearly Tyra wasn't a couch potato, judging from her firm bottom and effortless climb up the ladder each time they had to move it. Did she work out? Run? Do yoga? None of his business. Neither was the tempting shape of her body. But now that she'd admitted her interest, his brain was on a single track racing toward a broken trestle over a thousand-foot ravine.

Had Rance just called out something from the bandstand? Could have, but between the music and his sensual fog he couldn't be sure. He looked over there and his kid brother stood watching him, his eyebrows lifted as if expecting a response of some kind. "What? I couldn't hear you."

Rance stepped up to the mic and turned it on. "Can you hear me now?" Then he grinned.

"Yes, we can hear you now. You can turn that off."

"Do I have to? I've wanted an excuse to come up here and talk through the mic for ages. I like it. Maybe I could be some kind of emcee or something. Like on Valentine's night."

"Emcee of what? It's not like we have a set program we're following."

"Why not? You could do giveaways every fifteen minutes. That would spice things up."

"You know, Clint, that's not a bad idea." Tyra climbed down and he hoisted the ladder into a new position.

"You mean something like gift certificates to the Buffalo?"

"That, plus I could go around to the various businesses in town and see if anybody else wanted to add a gift. Your mom would probably throw in something from L'Amour and More."

"She will," Rance said. "Be sure and tell her it was my idea. See how this is shaping up?"

Tyra laughed. "I'll tell her. And thanks for coming up with it. It'll be simple to have people put their names and numbers in a bowl when they come in."

"True," Clint said, "but if they have to be present to win—"

"They won't. I'll be in charge of contacting winners who've already left, but people do tend to stay longer when the atmosphere is festive."

"You've got the festive under control." Clint handed her another garland when she was partway up the ladder. "These look amazing. I wouldn't have thought covering the wall surface with strings of hearts would make such a difference, but it feels like a whole other venue."

She beamed at him. "Doesn't it? I haven't had this much fun since decorating the gym."

"Hey, folksies." The mic squealed. "Back to the raffle—"

"It's not a raffle," Clint said. "That's when you try to raise money by making people pay for a ticket. This will be more like a series of door prizes."

"Okay, whatever. I get to draw winners and announce them, right?"

"Yes, you can." Tyra gave him a nod. "Since it's your idea, that seems fair."

"Just so you don't turn it into *The Price Is Right*, bro. This is supposed to be a romantic evening, not a game show."

"Don't worry. I'll keep it classy. I could wear my riverboat gambler vest. Might lift some weights between now and then so I'll stretch the material a little."

Clint snorted.

"Make fun if you want, but I notice you haven't snagged a sweetie in a while, big brother. Get some weights and buy you a vest and you'll improve your chances."

The ladder trembled slightly, as Tyra adjusted her position. Chances were good she'd done it so she could smother her giggles without Rance catching on.

"Thanks. I'll take it under advisement. So is the giveaway what you wanted to bring up when you tried to get my attention a while ago?"

"Heck, no. That there was a bonus brainstorm. Here comes another flash of brilliance. I've looked through all the bags and I didn't find any of those little guys wearing diapers."

"Are you talking about Baby New Year? That was last month." Clint had counted on Rance being a good distraction, but somebody must have put a quarter in him this morning because he was outdoing himself in that department.

"No, I mean the ones with the wings and bows and arrows. What are they called, again?"

"Cupid," Tyra called down from her perch. The answer came out with a slight quiver.

Clint looked up and met her gaze. She pressed her lips together. Yeah, she was about to lose it. Her color was high, which brought out the sparkle in her green eyes. "Did you buy any Cupid decorations?"

She shook her head.

"Looks like we won't have those in the mix, Rance. The lights look great though, don't they? And these garlands lining the walls?"

"You bet! I can hang the sparkly hearts from the chandeliers if you want."

"That would be perfect, Rance." Tyra came partway down to grab another garland from Clint's outstretched hand. "Sorry about the lack of Cupids."

"That's okay. Mom has some hanging up in the bookstore. Lucky and I helped her with those Sunday morning. She has extras, doubled her order without realizing it. She'd be happy to share them, I'm sure. I figure they should hang over the bar. That's where most of the arrow-shooting takes place, anyway. Alcohol is a good medium for flying arrows."

"Very true." Tyra winked at Clint. "Oh, before you put up those hearts, would you please hang the Valentine wreath on the door and put the crown on the buffalo?"

"Yes, ma'am." He flicked off the mic, hopped down from the bandstand and picked up the large wreath lying on a table. "Be right back."

The minute he was out the door, Tyra scurried down the ladder. "You did the right thing, inviting him to help decorate and it's been entertaining as hell, but he shouldn't be here when you try out the new buffalo greeting. He's too smart. He'd start asking why you were so involved with it."

"Let's send him to the bookstore to pick up the Cupids he's so eager to add to the mix. Unless you left Cupid out of this project for some reason. You don't have to put them up just because Rance wants them."

"I have nothing against hanging a few over the bar. I just didn't see any I liked when I was searching online last year. It was cute what he said about alcohol being a good medium for flying arrows."

"Ever been hit by one?"

She looked startled. "You mean like an instant attraction, where you meet someone and bingo, that's it?"

"Something like that."

"I never have. I guess my feelings take a long time to germinate. How about you?"

"Only once. Long time ago."

"Did it work out? Well, I suppose not since you're still single."

"That I am. I guess nothing ever worked out for you, either."

"You know, I was getting serious about a guy back in D.C. Then Dad dropped his bombshell and I told this man, let's call him Tony, that I had to pull up stakes and move back home and he was welcome to come with me. I said we could do some great things for the wildlife in Montana and actually have a chance to observe it, too."

"Let me guess. Tony declined that wonderful offer."

"Turns out he's petrified of wildlife."

Clint grinned. "Tony's loss. Our gain."

"Wreath's up." Rance came through the door, bringing a blast of cold air with him. "Still freezing out there. Now I'll tackle the buffalo's crown."

"Instead of that," Tyra said, "would you be willing to drive over to L'Amour and More and pick up those Cupids?"

"Sure can!" He settled his hat more firmly on his head and buttoned his jacket. "They're pretty cute. Chubby cheeks, a gleam in their eyes, like they can't wait to use that bow on you."

"If they're good enough for Desiree, they're certainly good enough for me. Thanks, Rance."

"Can I tell Mom about the giveaways?"

"Absolutely. That's one less stop I'll have to make."

"See you in a few. Don't have too much fun while I'm gone, okay?" He started for the door. "Oh, wait." He turned back. "I was supposed to ask you something, bro. Mom's hoping some of us can gather for dinner tomorrow night to finalize the birthday plans. I'm scheduled to work, but are you available?"

"I'm working that night, too, but if it's an early dinner, I could be there for an hour or two."

"She mentioned making it early, five or so."

"Then tell her I'll be there."

"Will do." Rance headed out the back door.

Don't have too much fun while I'm gone, okay? No chance of that. Clint turned around, took one glance at Tyra's face and paused. She looked panic-stricken. "Are you okay?

"Yes." She pivoted away.

"You're not acting okay."

"Better get that flash drive and do your thing." Her voice trembled. "You don't want Rance to catch you—"

"It'll take me five minutes and he'll be gone for at least twenty. More like thirty since he'll take time to brag about this awesome idea. Please tell me why you're so upset. Is it because we're alone?"

"Not really." She still wouldn't look at him.

"Then what?"

"It's too embarrassing."

"Tyra." Thumbing back his hat, he closed the gap, put his hands on her shoulders and gently coaxed her to face him. Sure enough, her cheeks were flushed. "If you'll tell me, maybe I can fix it."

"You could fix it, all right." She kept her attention on the floor.

"Then tell me."

She sucked in a breath. "Listening to Tim and Faith is a painful reminder that nobody's held me, nobody's kissed me, in two long years. And there you are, a guy I'm dying to kiss, and now we're alone and I want you to kiss me so bad it hurts." She lifted her head.

He gazed into the stormy depths of her eyes and his heart stuttered. "I would love to fix that for you."

"But you can't, because you and I—"

"I know." He drew her in, his blood pounding through his veins. "But a passionate woman should never have to go two years without being kissed."

"I'm thirty-five years old. I've surveyed the field, and the good guys are all taken."

Sliding an arm around her waist, he tucked her in close. Ah, she felt good. "Did you just insult me?"

"Except you, but I can't have you."

"Not on a regular basis, but you can have one kiss to tide you over."

She nestled against him and rested her palms against his chest. "Not a good idea." But judging from the glow in her eyes, the rest of her was in favor of that plan.

"No one ever has to know."

Her breath hitched. And her lips parted.

"I can keep a secret if you can." He slowly lowered his head.

With a gusty sigh that made her tremble, she wrapped her arms around his neck and tilted her head back. "Then do it."

Not the most romantic invitation he'd ever received, but so what? He'd dreamed about this moment since he was fourteen. He wasn't going to be picky about the details. Tim and Faith were on the sound system and Tyra was in his arms. Closing his eyes, he brushed his lips across hers.

She quivered. Swallowed.

He settled down and her breath caught. He'd touched a live wire once. This was like that, energy shooting through him, up to his head and down to his toes. But this live wire brought no pain, only a rush of pleasure so intense he groaned and dipped his tongue inside her hot mouth, desperate to taste, to submerge himself in the lush experience of kissing Tyra.

Peppermint and coffee. And something deeper, darker, a fire raging under the surface. He ached to reach it. Cupping her cheek, he slid his thumb into the corner of her mouth, wanting access to all that glory she'd buried for so long.

She opened for him, tightened her hold around his neck, rose on her toes, slid her curvy body higher on his. Oh, Lordy. Before he could stop himself, he'd spread both hands under her sweet bottom and lifted her up against his fly. She didn't hesitate, wrapping her legs around his hips. Didn't stop there. She hooked her ankles together and pressed hard against his swelling cock with a moan of frustration.

Gasping he forced himself to raise his head. "Damn, Tyra."

She met his hot gaze with one of her own. "Damn, Clint."

"We...we need to talk about this."

"You think?"

"I need to put you down."

"Go ahead."

"I would, but my fingertips are welded to the seat of your jeans."

"Well, I'm glued to your zipper. So there."

His breathing slowed a fraction, just enough to pick up the sound of a truck pulling in out back. "Somebody's here." That loosened his grip right quick.

"Yikes." She unhooked her ankles. "Put me down easy. I might be a little wobbly."

"Sure thing." He wasn't all that steady, either. He put his back to the rear entrance to shield her and hide his woody in case the person hotfooted it in here. "It's likely Vern, coming in to do some baking before we open. If it's Vern, he doesn't move like lightning."

"That'll help." She glanced down. "You're already company worthy."

"Panic has that effect."

"How do I look?"

"Fine, except your face is really flushed."

"I'll head up the ladder so he can't see that as well. Hand me another garland."

"The bag's empty. I'll have to get—"

"Then I'll fake it." She scampered up the ladder just as the back door opened and Vern strolled in.

He paused and looked around. "Hey, the place looks great!"

"Thanks, Vern!" Tyra called down from the top of the ladder.

"She deserves all the credit." Clint resisted the urge to tuck his shirt in before turning toward Vern. The tails weren't hanging out, but the extra material above his belt indicated he'd been doing something other than hanging garlands. "I've just been following orders, doing whatever she tells me." Wasn't that the truth. And now he was faced with the consequences of that out-of-control kiss. Could they go on as if it had never happened? They'd have to, wouldn't they?

"Well the customers are going to love this." Vern unzipped his jacket. "Great job, both of you. And I'd better get going. Those cakes won't bake themselves. And don't forget, Clint, we've got folks coming in to interview later."

"Three, right?"

"Yessir. I hope we end up hiring somebody 'cause I sorely need help in the kitchen."

"I'm sure one of them will work out."

"Hope so. Carry on." With a wave, he ducked into the kitchen.

Tyra came back down the ladder and glanced at Clint. "He didn't suspect anything."

"Nope. He can't hide his reactions worth a darn. We're safe."

"You'd better take care of the buffalo greeting."

"I'm on it." He glanced at her. "We'll talk."

"Definitely. I don't know what I expected, but that was—"

"Yes, ma'am, it certainly was." The kiss of a lifetime.

6

Those were the last private words Tyra exchanged with Clint all day. Rance came back with four adorable Cupids, each about twenty inches tall and perfect to hang above the bar without overwhelming the space. After Clint reported that the buffalo greeting worked, he retreated to the office claiming paperwork duties. That was fine with her. She and Rance easily finished up the decorating before the first customers arrived.

Everyone raved about the transformation. As customers filled the tables for the lunch meal, the familiar routine put the kiss in perspective. It wasn't like they'd ripped off their clothes and had sex on the floor. *But it was on the list, wasn't it, girlfriend?*

Good thing she hadn't been the only one going out of her mind. Clint had been as shocked by his response as she'd been by hers. She had an excuse — her recent celibate lifestyle — but surely Clint wasn't in that same boat.

Or was he? Rance had referenced Clint's lack of female companionship recently. Had he dated anyone since she'd taken over the Buffalo? Not that she'd noticed. Maybe that explained everything. They were both dry tinder looking for a match.

She spent the afternoon gathering gift certificates from local businesses. She returned at four, usually a slow time. Sure enough, Clint was in the office at his desk, his hat and jacket hanging on hooks next to the door.

When she walked in, he glanced up and smiled. "Hey, there. Any luck with gift certificates?"

"Tons. Everybody loved the idea. Have a minute?"

"Yes, ma'am." He saved whatever he'd been doing on the computer and turned his swivel chair to face her.

She reached back and gently closed the door. The soft click sounded loud in the silence. She turned back to him.

He'd left his chair and his expression had changed from relaxed to alert.

"Do you think I'm about to ask for another kiss?"

"It crossed my mind."

"I'm not." Her heart raced but she wasn't going to compound the situation by kissing him again. She might want to, but she still had some self-control. "Let's sit."

"All right." He waited for her to turn her chair around and sit down before he returned to his seat.

She gulped. Every move he made created a gravitational pull in his direction. His mouth was set in a grim line and she longed to say something that would make it soften into that smile that sent warmth surging through her veins. What a beautiful man. And she'd caused him distress.

The light in his blue eyes shifted. The wariness eased and that caring look she treasured took its place. "I'm so sorry, Tyra. I never should have kissed you. Instead of settling you down, I've stirred you up."

"What about you? Are you calm, cool and collected?"

"No, ma'am."

"I owe you an apology, too. And a solution."

His eyebrows lifted. "You've come up with one?"

"I'm a lawyer. That's what I do."

His laughter startled her.

"You think that's funny?"

"I think it's hysterical." He grinned. "Never occurred to me you'd analyze this like a difficult court case. I can't wait to hear what you came up with."

"It's obvious, judging from the way I responded to you this morning. I desperately need to find myself a boyfriend."

"A boyfriend?"

"It's a ridiculous label. Like we're back in high school. But society hasn't come up with anything better. And while we're discussing this, I might suggest you start looking for a girlfriend."

He shifted in his chair. "Don't have time. And by the way, I prefer women to girls."

"I prefer men to boys, but it's only semantics. We—"

"There's a perfect word, you know. It's even gender neutral. It's *lover*."

Thanks for dousing me with a bucket of lust. Taking a steadying breath, she scrubbed the erotic images of a naked Clint from her mind. She could handle this without blushing. "All right. We're adults. Clearly we both are wound tight. We each need to find a *lover* and work off some of this inconvenient sexual energy."

"Gonna go online?"

She shuddered. "Kill me, now."

"You said all the good guys were taken, so what's your plan?"

"I was hoping you'd help me brainstorm."

"*What?*"

"I've been away for years. Wagon Train is a small town, and after my lunch with Rachel I'm convinced that most men in my age bracket have found someone by now. I could be wrong. I'll bet you know everyone in town. Am I wrong?"

He scrubbed a hand over his face and sighed. "There's some truth to your evaluation." He paused. "Although...."

"You know of someone?"

"Hell, Tyra, I'm no matchmaker. I have no clue if—"

"You've thought of someone. I can tell. Who is it?"

His next sigh was heavier than the first, clearly weighed down with misgivings. "When Cheyenne moved in with Kendall last year, he rented his cabin to a friend in the fire department."

"Another firefighter?"

"Yes, ma'am. Dallas was a little shy about joining in family activities, but Christmas took care of that. We talked him into being part of the sleigh ride down Main Street caper and that broke the ice. We've assimilated him. He's one of us now."

"He was part of the group Christmas Eve?"

"Sure was. Tall guy, brown eyes, dark curly hair."

"I don't remember anyone like that. How old is he?"

"We threw him a birthday party last October. He turned thirty-two."

"And he's available?"

"Couldn't say for sure. He hasn't brought anyone to family events, but that doesn't mean he's not dating someone. I'd have to ask Cheyenne."

"Would you be willing to do that?"

"Yes, ma'am." He reached for the phone he'd left on his desk. "You know this is weird, right? I just kissed the living daylights out of you and now I'm trying to set you up."

"Quietly."

"You don't want anybody to know you're looking?"

"I'd rather not. I have this reputation in town as a powerhouse."

"A reputation you fully deserve."

"But a powerhouse shouldn't need any help in this area. I'd rather the word didn't get around."

"It won't. But this could be a dead end. You might not get along at all."

"Do you like him?"

"Very much. He's as solid as they come."

"That's good enough for me."

"Then here goes." Clint tapped out a message on his phone and sent it. "Not sure what

Cheyenne's schedule is today, but—well, there's your answer. Dallas isn't involved with anyone right now."

"Perfect. When can I meet him?"

"Let me check." He sent another message, then glanced at his phone. "He'll be there for the family dinner tomorrow night. Mom's been bugging me to ask you out to one of those dinners." He met her gaze. "Is tomorrow night soon enough?"

She breathed in. "Yes. Thank you."

"I'll take you out there and bring you back."

"That's not necessary."

"But it's practical. You've never been to Rowdy Ranch and it's a long drive along a road without a whole bunch of lights. Lots of icy patches this time of year and I'm familiar with them. We won't be there long since I have to work, but two hours should give you enough time to evaluate the situation."

"Then I accept." She pushed back her chair and stood. "I really appreciate this."

He rose to his feet. "Your wish is my command."

"What about you? Want me to start keeping an eye out for a likely candidate for you?"

"No, thank you."

"Maybe if this works out with me and Dallas, you'll be inspired to make the effort."

He gave her a crooked grin. "Gonna show me how it's done?"

"Something like that. I'd love to see you matched up with someone." And she would, damn it. He was terrific. He should have someone special in his life.

"Don't hold your breath."

7

Breathe, girl, breathe.

"You okay over there?" Clint took his eyes off the road for a couple seconds to glance across at her.

"I don't think I've ever been on a blind date. I'm nervous." She'd had a whole day to obsess about this evening and she'd worked herself into a lather.

"You're still not on a blind date. Those are terrible. We're simply going to dinner at Rowdy Ranch. You'll get to see Maverick. That little girl has taken a real shine to you."

"I've taken a real shine to her, too. Okay, I'll concentrate on getting to hold Maverick. That helps."

"And there's little Zach."

"He's adorable. Can't wait to see him again."

"Kids make great ice breakers."

"They do, at that."

"Not to mention you know everybody out there."

"Except Dallas."

"You might recognize him once you lay eyes on him. Come to think of it, he was in the bachelor auction last spring. He wasn't as terrified as Cheyenne but he still had to psyche himself up to do it. I can't recall what music he used."

"I mostly remember the drama with you and Cheyenne." And Clint's sexy cowboy swagger on that stage. She'd figured out the subterfuge and had made sure she was on hand for his dance. No other man had registered on her personal Richter scale that evening. Or since.

He'd taken time tonight to grab a quick shave before they'd left the Buffalo. The spicy scent of his favorite cologne reignited the fire from yesterday morning's kiss, when he'd also been freshly shaven.

She couldn't make herself regret that kiss, the only one she was ever likely to get from him. Tonight's dinner was designed to turn her attention elsewhere, but Clint would be at the table, too. Would she be able to shift her gaze away from him long enough to spend time looking at Dallas?

"I can hear you hyperventilating, again."

"Men have always sought me out. I've never deliberately tried to seek them out."

"Trust me, boss, this'll be more fun than you think."

Boss. She was beginning to detest that word. It stood between her and the man she craved. "How do you feel about calling me that?"

He stretched his arms, pushing against the steering wheel. "Honestly? I do it to remind myself, to keep things in perspective. Does it bother you?"

"It didn't before. I kinda liked it. Sounded cute coming out of your mouth, with a little teasing lilt to it. But now..."

"Now it feels like another brick in the wall."

"Yes." She leaned back against the headrest. "I spent time today rereading a section on employee/boss relationships in one of my business management books."

"And?"

"They're very clear it's a mistake to get involved. But playing devil's advocate, what would be so terrible about us becoming lovers?"

His breath hitched. "You tell me."

"We have a great working relationship now, but could we extend that relationship to the bedroom without messing things up?"

"You want to be the boss in there, too?"

"No, of course not. We would interact as equals."

"Glad to hear it. I had a sudden image of performance reviews."

"Oh, for heaven's sake."

He shifted into a falsetto. "Excellent work on the foreplay, Clint, but next time hold on another ten seconds, okay? I nearly didn't make it. And cuddle time was—"

"You're terrible."

"Really? I thought I sounded just like you."

"You sounded nothing like me. And for your information, the employer-employee dynamic would disappear during personal time."

"AKA sex."

"Not just sex. Other times. Like sharing meals."

"No limits on cookies?"

She groaned.

"You were kind of bossy about those cookies."

"Are you ever going to let me forget that?"

"Not if it nets me more cookies."

"I'm trying to make a serious point here. Let's say we become lovers."

"Let's say that."

"And then we go back into the office the next day and everything's changed."

"Somebody rearranged the furniture?"

"You know what I mean. Will we be able to switch back to our more formal interaction? Or do the lines of communication get sloppy because now we know each other in a whole other way?"

"I take it you've never been in this situation before."

"Never. Have you?"

"No, ma'am. Your dad's the only boss I've ever had until you came along."

She looked over at him, his strong profile visible in the light from the dash. "Was he a good boss?"

"He was. Not as cute as you."

"Thanks. I'll bet our styles are different."

"For sure. He wore his hair a lot shorter than you and he favored vests. I've never seen you wear a—"

"Can you be serious for five seconds?"

"Where's the fun in that?"

"I'm curious about something and I'd appreciate it if you'd give me a straight answer."

"Shoot."

"Why the Buffalo? It's obvious you love the place, but was it always your goal to work there and eventually become the manager?"

"Always. In fact, if you hadn't come back to take over, I would have mortgaged myself to the hilt and bought the place myself."

She stared at him, open-mouthed. "You never told me that."

"It became a moot point. You wanted it and you should have it. Your legacy, your childhood second home. Just so I get to continue to work there, it's all good."

"You'll have a job there as long as I have anything to say about it."

"Which you do."

"But, again, what's the big pull?"

"My dad. Cheyenne's and my dad, to be more specific. He loves it there and he instilled a love of the place, especially in me. He respects the history of the building, the way it serves as a hub for the community. He sees it as an establishment that helps hold the town together. When he visits, that's the first place we hit. Started when we were around three, old enough to sit at the table with booster seats."

"Has he visited since I moved back? I don't remember you mentioning it."

"He's had a couple of rough financial years and hasn't been able to make it to Wagon Train. He's an actor, which is always a rollercoaster."

"Would I know his name?"

"Probably not. He's managed to earn a decent living by working steadily, but he never hit the big-time. Some stunt double gigs left him with a few aches and pains. He was married three times and says that's enough. The last couple of years he's found work in Europe, which made it tough to come see us. He's hoping to visit soon, maybe in the next month or so."

"He sounds like a fascinating guy."

"Matter of fact, he is. Anyway, he's the reason I fell in love with the Buffalo." He pulled up in front of a low-slung ranch house with an expansive roofline that indicated massive square footage inside. The large snow-covered front yard sparkled in the glow of white lights in the surrounding trees.

"Clint, this is gorgeous. Does your mother always have lights in the trees?"

"She loves them. At Christmas she puts up even more, but she keeps the ones in the trees year-round. She likes living in a fairyland. Our house has been sparkly for as long as I can remember."

Her throat tightened. "You really are lucky."

"And I know it." He shut off the motor. "Let's go in, pretty lady."

"I like that way better than boss."

"Not calling you that anymore tonight. I've switched over to personal time."

8

Clint had dated plenty of women over the years, and not a single one had probed his reasons for his devotion to the Buffalo. No reason to. Waiting tables had been a logical first job for an eighteen-year-old and it might appear he'd fallen into the rest — bartender, head bartender and finally manager. When all along it had been according to plan.

It made sense that Tyra would ask because she'd observed his behavior more closely than most, but still, he was impressed that she gave him credit for being a planner instead of someone who drifted through life. She certainly didn't, and it was one of the traits that had drawn him to her from the beginning.

He didn't take her hand as they walked up the recently shoveled walk to the front porch. Bringing her tonight could give the wrong message to Dallas, so he'd better make sure he gave no indication there was anything between them. Which there wasn't. One lollapalooza of a kiss notwithstanding.

"I like what you said about the Buffalo." She climbed the steps, her boots hitting the treads in concert with his. "I recognize how much it means to me, but I'm not sure I've considered how much it means to the town."

"It was one of the reasons Mom decided to live here. She'd grown up in Apple Grove. The Choosy Moose plays a similar role in that town, at least so I hear from her and from Sky and Beau. I keep meaning to take a drive over there and check it out."

"Me, too. We should go together and take notes. We might pick up some ideas for the Buffalo."

"A business trip?"

"That was my thought."

"It's a good one." Forty-eight hours ago he wouldn't have hesitated. Now he saw a trip like that as a minefield, but evidently she had no concerns. She must really be counting on this Dallas situation to solve the problem.

He crossed the porch and reached for the large handle on the front door.

"Wait. What's his last name?"

He didn't have to ask who she was talking about. "Armstrong. Dallas Armstrong."

"Does he have any kin in Wagon Train?"

"Not that I know of, but that would be a good conversation starter."

"Right. You're right." She glanced up at him, a hint of anxiety in her green eyes. "Wish me luck."

"You know I do." He wished her a whole lot more than luck. He wanted her to be happy. If Dallas could bring her that happiness, he was all for it. Opening the door, he ushered her inside.

Sam, his mom's Lassie look-alike, stood just inside the door, bright-eyed and eager, his tail fanning the air.

"Well, hello, there." Tyra crouched down to pet him. "Aren't you handsome?"

"Mom named him Sam after John Wayne's sidekick in *Hondo*."

"That sounds like something your mom would do."

"Oh, does it?" His mother came out of the kitchen, all smiles, looking sharp as always in a forest green sweater and jeans decorated with bling. "Tyra, you finally made it out here."

"I can't believe it's taken me so long." Tyra stood and clasped his mom's outstretched hands. "I've heard so much about the place."

"Well, now that you know the way, I hope you'll make it a regular thing. I can't wait to show you my mini version of a Western bar. We're having dinner out there. Maverick and Zach will be so excited to see you. Ditch your coat and follow me."

Clint helped Tyra off with her coat out of habit. *She's not your date, dude. Don't be fetching her drinks and such.* He and Sam trailed the two women, who were deep in conversation about the two babies as they all trekked through the sprawling house to the newest addition, Rowdy Roost.

Not surprisingly, Tyra went nuts over the antique bar, the saloon-style tables and the myriad games available. "It's a wonder your family parties anywhere else."

His mom laughed. "They might not if I had a live band every night. Which would be ridiculous.

We all adore dancing at the Buffalo, so you won't get rid of us anytime soon."

"Well, as I live and breathe, if it isn't Tyra Lindquist." Beau sauntered over, his six-month-old daughter perched in his arms. "Maverick's been wondering if you'd ever show up here. She's been bugging me about it, in fact."

"Hi, there, Maverick! Come on over here, sweetheart." Tyra held out her arms to the copper-haired baby, who launched herself with a squeal of pure toddler joy. Once in Tyra's arms, she reached up, patted her cheeks and made cooing sounds.

Clint stood transfixed by the love fest going on between Tyra and Maverick.

"It's not fair, y'know." Beau sidled over to stand next to Clint and lowered his voice. "Every time Jess and I bring that kid into the Buffalo, Tyra comes out with something or other to charm the pants off my daughter."

"You mean treats?"

"Nah, not food. She's not out to spoil Maverick's appetite. I appreciate that."

"I'm not surprised to hear she doesn't show up with candy. She's a no cookies before dinner person, too. But if it's not treats, then—"

"Watch her. See if she pulls something out of her pocket. Yep, there she goes, giving that baby a soft little whoozit or a whatzit she located online somewhere. I'll bet she has a stash of them in her desk. You didn't ever notice her doing that when we brought Maverick in?"

"Guess not."

Beau eased back a little and leaned closer to Clint. "If you ask me, your boss is itching to have kids of her own. She treats little Zach the same way when Molly and Bret take him to the Buffalo. She's building a fan club of babies."

"Nothing wrong with that."

"You might not say so if it was your kid she was dazzling, while you're just plain old dad, the guy who changes her diaper and makes her take naps."

Clint smiled. "Jealous, are you?"

"Ah, not really. I think it's cute as hell. You know me. Always stirring things up. But I don't think I'm wrong about Tyra. I predict she's looking to settle down."

"I wouldn't know. None of my business." And speaking of settling down, where was Dallas tonight? He was supposed to be... ah, there he was, playing darts with Cheyenne, Kendall and Gil.

"I'd say it is your business, bro. If she gets hitched, there's an excellent chance that guy will have at least something to do with the Buffalo. You could end up with two bosses instead of one."

"Maybe not. He could have his own thing going on." Like fighting fires, for instance.

"Maybe, but you still better hope she chooses somebody you get along with."

"I'm sure she will." What about his brother Gil? He was also single. Why hadn't he mentioned him to Tyra? Probably because Gil was only twenty-eight. And also because Gil was his brother. It might be a failing on his part, but he didn't want to fix Tyra up with one of his brothers. Too close to home. Come to think of it, had Beau ever dated her? "I can't remember if you ever took her out."

"Not me. I was a sophomore when she was a senior and then later she was only here for the summers, so I just never pursued the idea. Too complicated."

"What about Sky? He was only a year behind her."

"Nah. We talked about it once, but he didn't see any point in asking her out since from the beginning she was planning to live back East and do her lawyer thing. He was determined to choose a hometown girl."

"Except he didn't."

"No. Good thing Penny was willing to relocate."

So neither of his older brothers had a history with Tyra. No skeletons in the closet, so to speak. "Hey, not to change the subject." Precisely to change the subject. He wanted Tyra to be happy, but picturing her with someone else wasn't a lot of fun. "Have you figured out what you're getting Angie for her birthday?"

"I was thinking a gift certificate for one of those magnetic signs she can put on her truck to advertise her handywoman business."

"Great idea. Won't she need two, one for each side?"

"I suppose. Wanna chip in?"

"Definitely."

"Hey, Beau," Tyra called out. "I'm returning your adorable daughter." She approached, cuddling Maverick and kissing the top of her curly head. "As you can see, she has a new friend."

"A bright orange friend, looks like. Whatcha got there, girl?"

Maverick pulled a dinosaur-shaped soft toy out of her mouth and offered it, dripping, to her father.

"That's lovely, sweetie." Beau pulled a bandanna out of his hip pocket and wrapped it around the slimy toy as he settled both baby and her new treasure in his arms. "Thank you, Tyra. Very thoughtful."

"You're so welcome. Catch you guys later. Desiree and I are off to play some darts and meet the new guy."

After they left, Beau gave Clint a look. "Meet the new guy?"

"She hasn't been officially introduced to Dallas."

"I see." He glanced over at the dart game in progress. "I'm putting two and two together and coming up with a winning hand. She came out tonight with more than spoiling kids on her mind, didn't she?"

Clint held his tongue.

"She could do a lot worse than Dallas, if that's the plan."

"No comment."

"I notice you didn't decide to go play darts."

"Not in the mood."

"Then let's go shoot some pool. Lucky and Sky look like they could use some company over there."

"Gonna teach Maverick the finer points of the game?"

"The way she watches everything, she already knows all the moves. Once she can master holding a cue she'll be running the table on all of us."

"Is that true, little one?"

Maverick gave him a grin that showed off the tooth she'd recently acquired.

Clint laughed. "You're gonna be a sandbagger, too, I'll bet. Come see your Uncle Clint. Let's go watch your daddy lose at pool."

Beau handed over the warm little bundle. "Didn't notice that before, bro."

"Notice what?" He unwrapped the orange dinosaur, gave it back to Maverick and returned Beau's soggy bandanna.

Beau folded it and shoved it in his back pocket as if used to the routine. "You're as addle-pated about my kid as Tyra is. Getting a little broody, are you?"

"Not me. I'll let the rest of you supply Mom with grandchildren." He started toward the pool table. "Which reminds me. I heard a rumor Penny and Sky might be pregnant. Any truth to that?"

Beau looked smug. "I'm not at liberty to say. Just keep your ears open tonight and you might get the answer to that question. And one you haven't thought to ask." He tilted his head toward the dart game, where Kendall was scoring one bulls-eye after another.

"Kendall and Cheyenne?"

"Like I said, I'm not at liberty to say."

"If Cheyenne told you before he told me, he's in deep—"

"He didn't. The ladies have a hotline." He nodded toward the oversized checkerboard where his wife Jess had a match going with Penny. "I'm not supposed to know anything, but I can read Jess like the front page of the *Sentinel.* I'd be much obliged if you wouldn't tell her that, though."

"Understood." Clint struggled to take it all in. Sky and Penny had wanted a baby for some time and he was excited for them. But now his twin was going to be a father, too? That shook him. They were still newlyweds who'd tied the knot last October, for heaven's sake.

Then again, Bret and Molly's marriage was only weeks old, and they were determined to provide Zach with a brother or sister as soon as possible.

Babies were popping up everywhere. "Hey, Beau?"

"Yessir?"

"Are you and Jess trying for baby number two?"

"Not yet."

"Whew. I'm glad. My head was starting to spin."

"I'm the holdup. She'd be fine going for it now, but I've convinced her to wait a little longer. I'm the one who has to work through my fears."

"Too bad every woman doesn't have them as easy as Mom did."

"Yep. I had a one-sided picture, but Molly says she didn't have much trouble having Zach, so each time someone else goes through it just fine, it gives me comfort." He glanced at Clint. "You'll have your turn. It changes you, bro. Fundamentally changes you to become a father. Despite how rough Jess's labor was, I wouldn't trade the experience of being a dad for anything."

"I believe you." And envy was eating at his heart. On the far side of the room, Zach clutched a handful of Sam's hair to steady himself as he took a few wobbly steps. The collie moved ahead slowly, clearly mindful of the important role he was playing teaching the next generation to walk.

The clan was growing and changing while Clint was standing still. Ever since Tyra had come back, he couldn't seem to find time for dating. Was he really that busy? Or had her presence reminded him that she was the only woman he'd ever wanted?

He looked over at the dart game. Tyra was up, her concentration obvious in every line of her body. She was out to win that match. Dallas stood by, focused on Tyra with the dazed expression most men wore when confronted with Tyra for the first time.

Clint's jaw tightened. Dallas Armstrong had no idea who Tyra was, the strength she possessed or the vulnerabilities she'd buried deep. It would take the guy months to scratch the surface and years to understand what made Tyra who she was. Clint was miles ahead of everyone when it came to knowing her. For all the good it did him.

9

Two hours later, Tyra gave Desiree a hug at the front door. Then she crouched down to scratch behind Sam's ears and kiss him on top of his silky head. "What a fabulous evening." She stood and gazed at her hostess. "Thank you for including me."

"My pleasure. Like I said before, we'd all love to have you come out again soon. Sam would love it, too."

The collie wagged his tail and gazed adoringly at Tyra.

"That sounds great."

"Good party, Mom." Clint hugged his mother. "See you soon." He ushered Tyra out the door.

"I adore your family." Tyra breathed in the cool air as they started down the porch steps. "Your *growing* family, as it turns out! That was exciting, hearing about those babies on the way."

"I'd figured on Penny and Sky's news, but I had no clue about Cheyenne and Kendall until Beau dropped a hint tonight. That surprised me, although it shouldn't. Cheyenne's always wanted kids, and like he said, he's not getting any younger."

"Two more nieces! Your mom is thrilled about that. Here she had all boys except Angie, and now she'll have three granddaughters to spoil."

"And trust me, she will. I've never known a woman to be as crazy about babies as my mother. Girls, boys, doesn't matter. She loves them all."

"Then it's a good thing the grandkids are showing up."

"Yes, ma'am." He walked to the passenger side of his truck, opened the door and offered his hand.

She took it. He'd probably made the gesture automatically, forgetting for the moment that she wasn't his date. His firm grip sent tingles through her body that she did her best to subdue, just as she'd worked hard to ignore him during the festivities. Judging from his laughter and lively conversation with his family, he'd had a terrific time, too.

He climbed quickly behind the wheel and started the engine. "How'd it go with Dallas?"

"You couldn't tell?" She crossed her arms and huddled against the cold seat as she waited for the cab to warm up.

"I wasn't really paying attention."

"We got along fine. He's a very nice guy."

"See there?" He backed the truck out and pulled away from the house. "All the nice guys aren't taken, after all. Gonna see him again?"

"We're having lunch at the Buffalo tomorrow."

"Lunch? Not dinner and dancing?"

"He suggested cooking me dinner at his house… or rather, Cheyenne's house, but I thought we should start with lunch at the Buffalo."

"Slow-playing it, I see."

"Well, yeah. I mean, I just met the guy. I'm not quite ready to be alone in his house with him."

"I promise you he's not the pushy type. He wouldn't do anything that you—"

"I'm sure he wouldn't. But dinner at his house would be more intimate than I'm ready for. Lunch tomorrow at the Buffalo suits me fine."

"If you say so. Seems like tonight was the equivalent of a lunch date, though. A follow-up meeting at your place of business seems overly cautious. But it's your call."

"Yes, it is. And while we're on the subject, why are you so eager for me to be alone with him?"

"Why are you so determined not to be?"

"Because when you accept an invitation for dinner at a guy's house, it's logical he will look for an opportunity to get romantic and I don't want to kiss him yet."

"Why not?"

"Because I just kissed you yesterday morning, okay? And I prefer a certain amount of time between that kiss and a potential one from Dallas. Like several days at least. More like a week or two."

"Hmm."

"Put yourself in my shoes. Let's say you just met an attractive woman tonight and spent the evening with her. Would you be inviting her over to your house tomorrow night with romance on your mind?"

"I might if I was trying to forget about kissing you."

"Are you?"

"Sort of."

"What do you mean *sort of*? Either you're trying to forget that kiss or you're not. Which is it?"

"I'm trying and failing." He glanced at her. "Happy now?"

"Of course not. I want you to forget it."

"It's not that easy, especially since I don't presently have anybody else I want to kiss. I can't just go randomly kissing someone. Not if I want it to be significant enough to override the one we had yesterday morning."

"I get that."

"In other words, I have zero candidates. Whereas you have Dallas waiting in the wings. I saw his face when he was watching you play darts. He'd be more than happy to kiss you."

"I thought you weren't paying attention."

"I wasn't. I just happened to see his face that one time."

"And how did he look?"

"Like every other guy when they first interact with you. As if someone just hit them upside the head with a two-by-four. You're a showstopper."

"Oh, for heavens sake!" Ah, but the compliment warmed her all over.

"Well, you are, and Dallas would be more than happy to engage in a lip-lock with you. He might be very good at it. He could probably make you completely forget about—"

"I'm not in the mood to kiss him. I need to be in the mood."

"I doubt you'll get in the mood sitting across the table from him at the Buffalo with folks all around talking and laughing. It's a cheerful atmosphere, but not what I'd call romantic."

"Are you kidding? The place is chock-a-block with hearts and Cupids."

"I guess there's that." He sounded ticked off.

And she owed him for suggesting she meet Dallas. "Don't get me wrong. I appreciate you setting this up for me. I'll take it from here. At my own pace."

"Absolutely. I was just surprised, since you clearly like him, that you—"

"Clint."

"Right. Case closed."

"Good." She glanced out the window. "Will we be driving past your house on the way home?"

"It's right up ahead. Why?"

"Just curious. I think it's cool that all of you have your own cabins sprinkled around the ranch."

"I won't argue with you, there."

"What's your cabin like?"

"It's made of logs, like everyone else's."

"But I'm sure you've added your own ideas to the design."

"I have."

"Like what, for example?"

"It's hard to explain unless you're looking at it. One of these days I'll give you a tour."

"You know, that would be fun. How about now? It'll only take ten minutes. The Buffalo will be fine without you for another ten minutes." And she could stretch out the time they'd be together. She'd enjoyed herself tonight, but she'd been mostly looking forward to the trip back with Clint.

He slowed the truck. "I suppose we could do it now."

"Makes sense to me. After seeing all the imagination your mom put into her place, I'd like to see what you did with yours. We could just pop in so I could take a quick look."

"Okay, sure. Why not?" He made a left and drove toward a sturdy log cabin. Snow covered the roof and a partially melted snowman stood in the front yard.

"Evidently someone was playing in the snow a few days ago."

"Bret, Molly and Gil brought Zach over. For some reason my yard had deeper snow than either Bret or Gil's. Wind direction, I guess."

"Was it Zach's first snowman?"

"Oh, no. He's been in on building several of them by now. But this was the day we taught him to make snowballs." Clint chuckled. "He wanted to make snowballs forever. Had to bribe him with cocoa to get him to stop."

"He's a neat little guy. Must be nice for all of you to live within a short drive of each other."

"Or a short horseback ride. Cheyenne's not as close anymore except by horseback. I miss having him right down the road from me. I used to stop by sometimes on my way home from the Buffalo."

"His place is nearby?"

"If you keep going down that road, it's the next cabin on the right. You can't quite see it from my house, but it's close, walkable in nice weather." He pulled up beside the porch steps. "You can get out here. That way you won't have to fight your way through the drifts."

"Thanks. That's gentlemanly of you."

"The McLintocks are known for it. Gentlemen R Us." He shut off the engine and opened his door. "I'll be around to meet you after I plow my way through the killer drifts on my side."

"I appreciate the sacrifices you're making." Sliding down to the bottom tread, she closed the passenger door and climbed the steps to the porch. It was empty of furniture. She turned back as he rounded the truck and took the steps two at a time. "Do you ever spend time out here?"

"Sure do. Brought the rockers in before the big snow, but I'll get 'em out again soon unless we're expecting another blizzard." Crossing the porch, he opened the door and ushered her inside.

"You don't lock it?"

"Hardly ever. None of us do. That said, we don't go barging into each other's houses without texting to see if it's okay."

Tyra breathed in the scent of a recent wood fire. "I love that cedar smell."

"That's mostly all I burn. Let's get some light on the subject." Closing the door, he made a circuit of the large living room, flicking lamp switches, one on either side of a massive sofa upholstered in red buffalo plaid. Two side chairs had the same pattern on the cushions.

"Buffalo plaid? On purpose?"

"Yeah." He smiled. "Corny, but then again, so's a talking wooden buffalo. Evidently I'm a fan of corny."

"Me, too." She gazed upward at beamed ceilings that gave the room a rugged, masculine vibe that matched the bold pattern of the cushions.

He turned on a third lamp sitting on a roll-top desk in the corner. Tyra looked closer at the two flanking the sofa. The base of each one had been carved from a thick piece of wood and embellished with a three-dimensional forest animal — a bear and a wolf on the ones flanking the sofa and a moose on the desk lamp.

"I love these lamps." She walked over and traced the outline of the wolf. "Did you find them in Missoula?"

"I made them."

She glanced up in surprise. "You...you *made* them?"

"It's a hobby." He shrugged. "Keeps me out of trouble."

"How could I not know you're a wood carver?"

"I don't tend to mention it. I'm a perfectionist, so it takes me forever to finish something. I've been working on a lamp for my mom since July and it was supposed to be a Christmas present. I might get it done for her birthday next August."

"Well, I'm impressed." She unbuttoned her coat. "How come you didn't put a buffalo on one of the lamps?"

"I let the plaid be the reference in here. A buffalo on one of the lamps would be redundant. I saved that for my bedroom. And in case you were wondering, my house isn't a carbon copy of Cheyenne's."

"I didn't think it would be. Just because you're twins doesn't mean you'd want the same house design."

"True. But it occurred to me you might have thought scoping out mine would give you a preview of what Dallas's will be like. Assuming you eventually have dinner there."

"Honestly, I didn't even think of that." Dallas was the last person on her mind at the moment. "But since you brought it up, how is yours different from Cheyenne's?"

"His is dominated by a rock fireplace on the wall opposite the front door. It's the first thing you see when you walk in, floor-to-ceiling rock. Beautiful. Pricy, too. My fireplace is a lot smaller and I used river rock. Smoother, not so dramatic. I put it on the kitchen wall and it's dual-sided so you can have a fire in both rooms. I stole that idea from Beau."

"That must be nice on a chilly morning."

"Makes the kitchen cozier, that's for sure."

"What else is different?"

"The bedroom layout. We each have a primary and a guest room, but his are on either side of the hall with a guest bath at the end of the house. I added square footage so I could have a big bedroom and bath across the back, kind of like a suite."

"Can I see it?"

He gazed at her for a second.

"Hey, if that's too private, never mind. You said the buffalo carving was in there, so I—"

"It is." He led the way down the hall. "I like having my bedroom at the back of the house, but that means the master bath is quite a ways from the rest of the plumbing. The water takes forever to heat up, so eventually I'll install an on-demand system to fix that." Opening a set of double doors at the end of the hall, he beckoned her inside.

She stepped through the doorway and sucked in a breath. The combination of virility and sensuality created a seductive atmosphere that made her quiver with longing. Clint might never admit that he had a romantic soul, but the evidence was everywhere she looked.

He must have spent months, maybe a couple of years on the tall wooden headboard. The forest scene included the same animals he'd carved into the lamps, with the addition of a handsome male buffalo at the center. Plump snowy pillows stacked against the headboard created just the right welcoming touch to soften the imposing majesty of the embellished wood.

The lamps on each nightstand had no animal images. Instead they were graceful spirals of cedar, gleaming and smooth. Their simplicity allowed the elaborate headboard to take center stage. A large, handmade quilt in a riot of colors covered the bed.

On the far side of the room, a cozy arrangement of two easy chairs and a small table faced an old-fashioned wood stove. Books lay on the table in no particular order. A knit throw had been tossed over the back of one of the chairs.

How many lucky women had he entertained in this fantasy bedroom? And why hadn't he ended up with any of them?

"And that's all the time we have, folks!"

His brusque announcement snapped her out of her daze. "You're kicking me out?"

"Yes, ma'am. Just head through the door to your right and make sure you take all your belongings with you. Feel free to tip your tour guide. He's working his way through the school of hard knocks."

"But I wanted to ask you about—"

"Tour's over." He gave her a jaunty smile. "Meet you out at the truck. I need to close up the venue." The grin was carefree, but the flash of lust in his eyes… not so much.

She quickly hurried out of the room, pulse racing. She'd figured he was immune to the sensual effect of his bedroom since he'd slept in it for years. Then again, he had hesitated when she'd asked to see it. "I'll…I'll just go get in the truck."

"That would be dandy." He turned off lights in the bedroom and started down the hall after her.

She picked up the pace and was out the front door by the time he made the circuit to shut off the lamps in the living room. The truck cab was still warm, but she was trembling. She closed the door as he emerged from the house.

Buckling her seatbelt with shaking hands, she sank back against the upholstery. Asking to see his bedroom had been a mistake, but she wouldn't have missed it for the world.

He swung up into the driver's seat and slammed the door. Then he gripped the wheel and stared out the windshield. "That was close. I almost grabbed you."

"It's my fault. I shouldn't have—"

"I should be able to give you a damned tour of my house without..." He shook his head. "But when you were standing by the bed, something shifted. I could feel your skin under my fingertips. I could taste you on my tongue. I could imagine the incredible sensation of making love to you, and I wanted that more than I wanted to breathe."

She hugged herself tight. It helped with the shakes. And stopped her from reaching for him. "I'm...I'm sorry. I just wanted..."

"I know what you wanted, Tyra. What you still want." He reached for the keys dangling from the ignition and started the truck. "So do I. But if it puts the business at risk—"

"Right. Thanks for the tour. I'll stay the heck out of your bedroom from now on."

10

Clint had just finished shaving the next morning when someone rapped on his front door. Scrubbing a towel over his face, he hurried into the bedroom and grabbed a T-shirt and jeans. A member of his family would have texted him before coming over.

He pulled on the jeans, buttoned and zipped them. Tyra? His stupid heart went crazy at the possibility that she'd pay him an unannounced visit this morning, especially after she'd vowed to stay away. But what if she'd tossed and turned the way he had? What if she'd decided after a sleepless night that they should go for it?

Barefoot, he tugged the T-shirt over his head on his way to the door. Stubbed his toe on the back leg of the sofa because he wasn't watching where he was going. Idiot. He swore under his breath, just in case Tyra was the person standing out there.

Toe throbbing and breathing like a freight train, he opened the door. It took him a second to erase the fantasy he'd carried to the door and replace it with reality. "Hey, Dallas."

"Sorry, did I catch you at a bad time?"

"No, no." He opened the door wider and stepped back. "What can I do for you?"

"I should've called first. But I saw the smoke from your fire so I figured you were up, and you don't usually drive into town until later, so I—"

"I was up." He closed the door against the icy air drifting in, although it felt good on his toe. "Can I get you some coffee?"

"That would be great."

"Come on in the kitchen." He led the way. "I'll stoke up the fire."

"This setup with the two-sided fireplace is awesome. I remember it from the last time I was here."

"I like it, especially first thing in the morning." He poured a mug full of coffee for Dallas and another one for himself. "I seem to remember you like it black."

"I do. Thanks." He took the steaming mug.

"Have a seat." Clint pulled out a kitchen chair and motioned to another one.

"I feel kinda dumb coming over here." Dallas took the chair Clint had indicated. "Probably why I didn't call. I was pacing the front porch, trying to decide whether to come over, and I saw your smoke. Smelled it, actually."

"You're probably good at that."

"Oh, yeah. This was a nice smell. When something's burning that's not supposed to—not such a nice smell."

"Right." He sipped his coffee and waited.

Dallas stared into his coffee mug for a little while. Then he looked up. "So I'm here about Tyra."

"Oh?"

"I was supposed to meet her for lunch today."

"Mm."

"You knew that, didn't you?"

"She told me on the drive back to town."

"Anyway, she texted me first thing this morning. Instead of meeting for lunch, she wants to take me up on my original offer to make her dinner at my house."

Huh? "Interesting."

"I made the offer because I go back on duty tomorrow, so I thought an at-home dinner would give us the best chance to get to know each other."

"Makes sense."

"But she seemed skittish about it. This morning she's all in. I wondered, since I know you're good friends, if you have any insight on why she changed her mind."

Clint gazed at him. What to say? Or more to the point, what *not* to say? Tyra had made it clear she wanted him to stay out of this situation.

"Listen Clint, if you don't feel comfortable talking about it, that's fine. I just figured since you've known her a long time and worked with her for the past couple of years...."

"She's an incredible woman." He could say that much without messing up the works.

"That's obvious. Jess told me she was a dynamo in high school and nobody was surprised when she became a lawyer. Last night Tyra mentioned that she's donating her legal services now that she has an income from the Buffalo."

"Yep. She wants to make the world a better place."

"And on top of that, she's beautiful."

"True." The image of her standing beside his bed still made him ache. "She hasn't dated in a while, though." Not exactly a secret to anyone who'd paid attention.

"I sensed that. A lot of caution going on."

"Ever since she moved back to Wagon Train, she's poured all her time and energy into running the business."

"I could tell she wanted to take things slow, which is fine, but when she changed her mind so quickly, I wasn't sure what to think."

"I'd still take things slow."

"Okay." He nodded. "This might sound weird, but it's almost like she's making herself do this. She likes me, but she's not into me, if you know what I mean."

"She doesn't believe in instant attractions. She has to get to know someone first, so if you give her time, who knows what might happen?"

"Good point."

"She's worth the wait."

"That I believe." He pushed back his chair and stood. "Thanks, Clint."

"Anytime." He offered his hand and Dallas shook it. "Good luck." Did he mean it? Yes, yes he did. Like Beau said, Tyra could do a lot worse than this guy, who had cared enough to seek advice about how to handle the situation.

Tyra might eventually discover that she was wildly attracted to Dallas and her interest in

Clint would start to wane. He wouldn't have to worry about making a mess of the job he loved.

11

Clint's toe felt better by the time he finished dressing. He was able to shove his foot into his boot without pain. Donning his hat and jacket, he picked up his keys, pocketed his wallet and left the cabin. Heading to town and the Buffalo had always been a pleasant prospect and it had become even more so in the past two years. Would that change if Tyra became involved with Dallas?

No. He'd be happy she'd found someone. She'd been out of reach his whole life and she still was. If she fell in love right in front of him, that should squash any lingering feelings he had for her.

The firefighter's black truck was still parked in front of Cheyenne's place when Clint drove past. The guy was likely inside deep cleaning the cabin in preparation for tonight. Maybe planning the menu, making a shopping list. Checking the expiration date on his condoms?

Clint swore softly. He had to get off that topic or he'd drive himself crazy. Why had Tyra agreed to this dinner, after all? He wanted to ask her, but that would mean revealing that Dallas had told him about it. Not cool.

She was in the office at her desk. If she'd had a restless night, she didn't show it. She'd worn her hair down and it gleamed in the overhead light. Her cream-colored sweater was one of his favorites. Sexy in a classy way.

She looked up from the computer. "Hey, there. Got a minute?"

"Sure. What's up?"

"Tom called a while ago. The Beat-Up Trucks can't play tonight and they might be out of commission for several days. Two guys came down with the flu and Jim and the drummer aren't feeling so good, either. Apparently this is a bad bug, and he advised me to find a replacement to make sure we have a band for our Valentine party."

"Any luck?"

"I located one called House Wine. Their venue in Missoula recently went out of business and they're looking for a gig, even a temporary one. They have good reviews and they're willing to drive down for an audition this afternoon. Would three o'clock work for you?"

"Yes, ma'am, I'll be here. That's too bad about the Trucks. Customers really like their sound."

"That's partly because they're so used to their style of playing after all these months. They've learned their names and have their favorites. If this group is decent, we should start them off tonight if they're willing. Maybe by Valentine's Day they'll have endeared themselves to the crowd just like the Trucks have."

"Good idea. It'll help if they're personable."

"Jim, the leader, was easy to talk to, so that's a good start."

"Agreed. Was there anything else?"

"Um, yes. I thought about what you said last night."

A tingle ran up his spine. "Which part?"

"The whole thing. I decided you were right. I was being a wuss about getting to know Dallas. I need to step out of my comfort zone. I'm having dinner at his place, after all."

He put on his poker face. "That's great."

"You don't look surprised."

"Why should I be? It makes sense that you'd reconsider after you had time to think it through."

"It's no big deal."

"I'm glad you see that."

"I'll relax, have a drink or two. If things heat up and I'm in the mood, I'll go with it."

"Good plan." Just wonderful. Now he'd probably spend the day visualizing what would be happening tonight in Cheyenne's cabin. Maybe he'd pick up a mouth guard at the drugstore so he didn't give himself lockjaw.

As it turned out, he had no time to torture himself about what might or might not happen during Tyra's dinner with Dallas. The interviews for kitchen help took more time than he'd budgeted, but at least he and Vern hired one of the three candidates, so his cook was happy.

He gobbled a sandwich for lunch and put in a couple of hours afterward with Rance inventorying the liquor supply and placing the necessary orders. When a group started setting up on the bandstand, he glanced at the antique clock on the wall. Three on the dot. House Wine was punctual, a point in their favor.

Tyra came over to the bar. "They'll be ready in about ten minutes. Can you take a break?"

"Yes, ma'am." He surveyed the tables. He'd let both servers take an hour off to run errands since the crowd was almost nonexistent. Other than his mother's book club members finishing a late lunch, the place was empty. "I'm gonna ask the Wenches to help us rate the band."

"Good idea."

"Hey, Clint." Rance tucked a bottle of rum back in its spot. "Since it's slow, can I sit in on the audition?"

Clint glanced at Tyra.

She shrugged. "I don't see why not. I figured we'd watch from a two top by the dance floor. I'll add an extra chair." She started in that direction, then swung back to face them. "Rance, if you'll get us each a cup of coffee, I'll ask Vern for three pieces of chocolate cake."

"Excellent!"

"Sounds good." Clint gave her a thumbs-up that earned him a smile before she turned and walked over toward the dance floor. Yeah, this was the easy relationship they needed to maintain. No tension, especially of the sexual variety.

Lifting the hinged portion of the bar, he made his way over to the table occupied by the Wenches Who Read, women he'd known all his life. His honorary aunties. His mom wasn't with them today, since she rarely went out to lunch when she was racing to meet a book deadline. Jess was the seventh member of the group, but between her job at the *Sentinel* and her six-month-old daughter, she had no time for leisurely lunches, either.

These five had retired, except for Cindy, who still worked a few hours a week as a hairdresser. As usual when they showed up as a group, they each wore their signature colors — yellow for Nancy, red for Colleen, orange for Teresa, indigo for Annette and blue for Cindy. Sometimes Clint would meet one of them in town wearing a different color and it always threw him.

"Hey, Clint, what's with the new group?" Colleen gestured toward the bandstand. "You're not replacing the Trucks, I hope."

"No, ma'am. Some of them are out sick, so Tyra and I are auditioning this outfit for temporary backup. They call themselves House Wine."

Nancy grinned. "Good name."

"Can you all stay for a while and have a listen? Give us your opinion before you leave?"

"You bet." Teresa glanced around the table. "Critiquing is what we do."

Annette looked at him. "Should we take notes? Or just give you a verbal critique?"

"Verbal's good enough. They either fit the Buffalo vibe or they don't."

"Speaking of the Buffalo vibe." Cindy fluffed her hair, colored bright red with white streaks for Valentine's month. "We all love the new greeting. Kinda sexy, actually."

"And we figure you have to know who recorded it." Teresa eyed him. "You can tell us. We're extremely good at keeping a secret."

"That's true, but I'm contractually obligated to protect that bit of information."

Colleen huffed. "You're no fun."

"He can be," Teresa said. "Like when he did that dance for the bachelor auction last year."

"You should be in it for real this year." Nancy gazed at him. "As yourself. Seriously."

"I'm not a firefighter."

Colleen rolled her eyes. "Insignificant detail. The idea is to raise money for the department. You should volunteer to do it. I'm sure they'd be happy to have you."

Teresa laughed. "And so would all the single ladies."

"I'll think about it." He'd had a good time, so maybe he should. "If you'll excuse me, I'd better go over and join Tyra and Rance. Thanks for helping us with the audition." He turned and started to walk away.

"Hey, Clint," Annette called after him. "Are we allowed to clap and stuff?"

He glanced back. "Of course."

"We could make cards with numbers, like in the Olympics," Colleen said. "I have a pad of paper in my purse."

"Uh, maybe not do that. This is an audition, not a competition."

"Okay, then." Colleen nodded. "We'll just stick with clapping. Or clapping politely if they're so-so."

"That's fine. See you in a few." Clint continued over to the table where Tyra and Rance sat across from each other with mugs of coffee and thick slices of cake. Rance's was nearly gone and Tyra had eaten about half of hers.

She gestured toward her plate. "We started on the cake without you."

"No worries. I didn't expect to be so long." He took a seat between the two of them and picked up his fork. "I hope I didn't create a monster by asking for their opinion."

"Why?"

"I didn't factor in how much they love judging. Colleen was ready to make numbered cards they could hold up after the band played something."

Rance grinned. "Whoops. Although that would have been funny."

"I told them not to." He dug into his cake. "They agreed to just clap, loud if they like it and soft if they don't."

"Ugh." Rance made a face. "I hate that polite clapping. I'd almost rather have someone booing than polite clapping."

"I think they'll like the band," Tyra said. "Anyway, Jim made a request of us."

"Oh?" He took a swallow of coffee. "What's that?"

"Since we hire a band for dancing and not just for background music, he'd like us to get out on the floor for a couple of the numbers to make sure their sound is something that'll work for us. I told him we're old hands at this, so he figures if we enjoy dancing to their music, so will the crowd we draw."

"I guess that makes sense."

"I offered to dance, too," Rance said. "I could ask the Wenches. But unless they play five songs, which is a lot, I'd have to leave some out and that wouldn't go over well, so I—"

"Rance and I decided he probably shouldn't get into it." Tyra covered a smile with her napkin.

"Good call."

"Also, you and I have the most experience dancing at the Buffalo."

"But not with each other." A quiver of excitement warned him this could be a bad idea.

"Does that matter? We're both good at it. We shouldn't have any trouble evaluating whether this band will encourage our customers to get out on the floor."

"All right. I'm game." If he balked, Rance would grab the chance in a heartbeat.

"We won't dance the first number, though. I told him we'd come out for the second one. So you get to finish your cake."

"Thanks. You know I love chocolate cake." But the next bite tasted like sawdust. Did she understand the inherent danger in this plan?

Evidently not. Maybe it was a simple physical exercise for her, similar to the cheerleading moves she'd executed in high school. If she treated it that way, he'd just follow suit.

Oh, hell, who was he kidding? Dancing with Tyra had been his dream for years. He'd milk it for all it was worth. The consequences be damned.

12

The band led off with Luke Bryan's *What Makes You Country.* Jim Nicholson, the band's vocalist, sure could sing, and Tyra tapped her foot in time to the catchy tune. When she looked over at Clint, he was tapping his fingers on the table. His mouth was curved up in a subtle smile and he gave her a quick nod. Rance bobbed his head to the beat, clearly happy with this rendition.

One song wasn't enough to know for sure the band would work out, but when it was over, the Wenches whistled and stomped. Rance did, too. Then he leaned across the table. "You should hire them. They're awesome."

"They're good, but we need to hear a little more." She glanced at Clint. "Right?"

"Definitely."

Jim thanked the small audience and tipped his hat to the Wenches. So the guy had charm as well as talent. Tyra's worry that she'd be left without a band on Valentine's Day eased.

Jim turned his attention back to Clint and Tyra. "Ready to get out here?"

Clint stood. "We are." He held out his hand to Tyra.

"Just to warn y'all, we're gonna ramp it up some."

"We can handle it." Tyra grasped Clint's hand and stepped onto the dance floor as the band launched into Travis Tritt's *Southbound Train.*

Clint laughed and swung her into his arms. His sure grip and perfectly coordinated moves sent her whirling around and spinning under his arm. His blue eyes flashed a challenge.

Challenge accepted. A jolt of adrenaline made her giddy, as if she'd pushed off at the top of a black diamond ski run. She'd never danced like this, propelled at a dizzying pace by a partner who had the flexibility of a gymnast and the stamina of a long-distance runner. She matched him step for step, galvanized by his energetic style, high on life, high on Clint.

The number was over sooner than she wanted it to be. The Wenches erupted, whooping and hollering. Rance whistled and cheered. She doubted it was all for the band, She and Clint had given a heck of a performance.

Gasping, she stood facing Clint, still enclosed in his arms, although he'd loosened his hold. "I loved that."

He was breathing hard, too. "It was fun."

"How come we've never danced together before?"

He smiled. "You never asked me."

"You could've asked *me.*"

"Didn't have the nerve."

"Don't be ridiculous. Like I would have turned you down."

"I didn't know that."

She searched his gaze. He wasn't kidding. "Well, I wish I'd asked you a long time ago. I've been missing out."

"I wish—"

"Hey, folks, we'd like to show you what we can do with something a little slower."

Tyra glanced up at the bandstand. Oh, yeah. They were supposed to be auditioning these guys. "Great." She turned back to Clint. "Want to dance this one?"

He hesitated.

"We don't have to. I think we know—" She was interrupted by the strum of the guitars.

"Let's dance it." He drew her close as Jim began singing Kenny Chesney's *Somewhere with You.*

The song had a jaunty beat, a danceable rhythm that could have become another wild ride. But Clint chose a different path. He did less swirling her around and more gentle movement, a sexy two-step that brought their bodies in contact. A lot. His hips brushed hers. His chest touched her breasts for a sweet, tantalizing moment. He was slowly driving her crazy.

And through it all, he held her gaze.

He was seducing her. No question about it. He knew it. She could tell by the glow in those mesmerizing eyes. If she looked away, she'd break that sizzling connection. She didn't.

The lyrics gradually penetrated the haze of arousal he'd created. The song was about a guy yearning for a woman beyond his reach. Had Clint recognized the song from the opening chords?

As the last guitar riffs faded away, he spun her slowly under his arm and pulled her close. "Thank you."

She was vaguely aware of the Wenches and Rance going ballistic but the look in his eyes was all she really cared about. "Did you know they were about to play—"

"Yes, I did." He kept his voice low. "Discovered that song when I was a freshman. Played it constantly that year. I'm guilty of giving in to a fantasy I've had for a very long time. I hope you'll forgive me." He let her go and stepped away.

"Oh." She couldn't figure out what to do next. Her first instinct, to grab him and kiss him like there was no tomorrow, was unacceptable. She wasn't supposed to crave this man, let alone engage in public smooching.

"I've made you uncomfortable. I apologize."

Now she knew what to do. She kept her voice down, too. "You don't have to apologize. That was the sexiest, most arousing dance experience of my life. I wouldn't have missed it for the world."

"Same here. But I—"

"Ma'am? Would you like us to play another tune?"

She faced the bandstand. "That's not necessary, Jim." She turned back to Clint. "Your opinion?"

"I recommend we hire them."

"I agree." She glanced back at Jim. "If you can start tonight, we'd be thrilled."

"Yes, ma'am! We can certainly do that."

"Terrific. My manager will handle the details. I...um...have some things to take care of." She made eye contact with Clint. "I'll see you in the morning."

He'd reverted to his poker face. "See you then."

13

Tyra was impressed. Dallas had knocked himself out. He'd fed her a delicious meal, asked intelligent questions about her work with wildlife preservation and entertained her with stories of growing up in a large, noisy family in New Jersey. He was the only one who'd moved out West. His family thought he was insane.

"I don't think you are." She gazed at him across the candlelit table he'd set up in front of the fireplace. He was nice to look at. Had a pleasant voice. "There are city folks and country folks. You might have been born a city boy, but clearly you belong in the country."

"That's for sure. I always wanted to be a firefighter, but even that didn't feel right when I was part of a big station in Trenton. A rural fire department suits me way better."

"I can see that." They'd lingered over dinner, sipping a very good wine. "Are you going to do the bachelor auction again this year?"

He made a face. "With luck I won't be a bachelor by then."

"Oh? Is there a special someone?"

He flushed. "No, I didn't mean it like that. And I didn't mean that I'm desperate to get involved with someone. I'm just... ready to settle down."

"So what qualities are you looking for in a partner?"

"Someone who's her own person. Who'll speak up about what she wants instead of going along with everything I say or do."

"An independent woman, then."

"Absolutely. One who's figured out what she wants to do with her life and she's doing it. Like you."

That made her smile. "I don't have my life figured out."

"Looks like it from where I stand." He gazed at her, warmth in his eyes. "I'll also admit that I'd like to have children."

"So would I." She'd never said it out loud, not even to Tony, and she'd been serious about him. He'd been the only man she'd considered marrying.

"Really?" He brightened. "I was thinking you might have decided against it."

"No. Just never found the right person."

Warmth shone in his eyes. "We have that in common."

"We have lots of things in common."

"We do, and that's why I—"

"I think we could become really good friends."

He regarded her quietly. "I think you're right. We get along great, but..."

"Something's missing."

"And yet on paper we're... well, to be fair, I haven't asked you what you're looking for, so maybe I'm the one who doesn't measure up."

"You tick all the boxes, Dallas. You love Wagon Train, find satisfaction in your work and have a great sense of humor. Heck you even know how to cook. On top of that, you're very easy on the eyes. I'm amazed you're still single."

"And I can't believe you're single." He grinned. "We're perfect for each other."

"Maybe that's the problem. We're so perfect for each other that it's boring."

That made him laugh. "Could be. We had it all tonight — candlelight, soft music, a flickering fire. If we can't generate chemistry under these conditions, we should probably give up."

"You set up a beautiful scene and I appreciate the effort you made."

"I enjoyed doing it. I like talking to you. It's been a nice evening."

"It has. Like I said, we're destined to be friends." She pushed back her chair. "Come on, let's clean up the dishes."

He stood. "I can't have you washing dishes. I can just pile them in the sink and we'll watch a movie or something."

"Let me help with the clean-up. That's what friends do."

"Okay, let's get this table cleared."

"Then we'll play checkers."

"Seriously?"

"You don't like checkers?"

"I love checkers, but—"

"Then that's the plan."

Two hours later, when they were tied in number of games won, she was ready to call it a night. "This has been fun, but I'm going home, now." She got up.

"It's late." He stood, too, and walked over to the coat rack. "I feel like I should drive you."

"That makes no sense. I need my truck to get to work in the morning and besides, you'd have a long round trip taking me home and coming back here. I'll be fine."

"At least I'll walk you out." He helped her on with her coat and grabbed his before ushering her out the door. "Cold out here."

"Yeah, it is."

"Thanks for your honesty." He gave her a hug.

"Thanks for yours."

"Text me when you're home safe."

She climbed behind the wheel. "I will." The truck started right up. Giving him a wave, she backed out of the parking spot and drove the short distance to the ranch road. Before she made the right turn, she switched on the radio. Faith Hill's *Breathe* was halfway through. She'd first heard it in middle school and hadn't fully understood it until much later.

Tonight it made her tingle. Making love with Clint would be like that. Why couldn't Dallas be the man who turned her on? Early in the evening she'd tried to talk herself into a sexual attraction. Didn't work. Wine didn't help. Gazing at him across a candlelit table had no effect, even with romantic music playing softly in the background.

Maybe she'd try to find Dallas a girlfriend. Now that he'd talked a little bit about his preferences, she might run into someone who would be right for him.

She sang along with Faith and let herself imagine she was in bed with Clint. He'd indulged his fantasies during that dance this afternoon so she could indulge hers, right? Looked like fantasies were all she'd—

Just as the song ended, the truck's engine cut out. What the hell? Pulling over to the side of the road as the truck glided to a stop, she switched the key to off and turned it back on. Nothing. Tried again. No response. The lights still worked so it wasn't the battery. *Fuel pump.* She heard her dad's voice in her head. He'd been stranded once just like this by a doggone fuel pump failure.

She'd probably have to call Dallas. He'd be glad to ride to the rescue. But then what? The truck couldn't be fixed tonight, so she'd have to spend the night at his house. She made a face.

They'd agreed to be friends, but that didn't mean he'd become a close enough friend that she'd feel comfortable sacking out in his guest room. If he even had one. He hadn't taken her on a tour, which was funny considering she'd practically demanded that Clint give her one.

Clint was her other option. She checked the time on her phone. He might still be at the Buffalo. Or he might have let Rance close up. In that case, he could be fast asleep in his beautiful bed.

Groaning, she flopped back against the headrest. "Truck, *you* are not my friend right now. Looks like I'll have to call Dallas, and you *know* I don't want to do it. How about starting for me, huh?" She turned the key again. Nothing. "All right. I'll call — wait...is that..."

Headlights bobbed in the distance, coming her way. Had to be a McLintock since they were the only ones who lived out here. Come to think of it, any McLintock would do. Desiree had that huge house which must have several spare bedrooms. Whoever was driving toward her could take her to Desiree's. Might have to wake her up, but this was a semi-emergency, so Desiree would be understanding.

She turned on her flashing lights to alert the driver that she needed help. The truck veered to her side of the road and pulled up facing her. For a moment the headlights blinded her. Then the driver switched to the parking lights, climbed out and walked in front of her headlights, flipping his collar up and zipping his jacket.

Clint.

14

Speak of the devil. Or rather, the angel. Clint had been focused on Tyra all the way home and here she was, pulled over with an issue. He put on his gloves as he rounded her truck and walked up to the driver's side.

She rolled down the window. "Fancy meeting you here."

"I think that's my line. What's up?"

"The engine cut out. Since I still have lights, I think it's the fuel pump."

"Good guess. Could be the alternator. If it was gas, I have a can in the back, but since it's not, we're looking at fixing it tomorrow." He opened her door and held out his gloved hand. "Might as well come get in my truck."

"Then what?" She tucked the keys in her purse and picked it up.

"We'll discuss that in the warm cab, okay?"

"Okay." She put her hand in his. "I'm glad you came along."

He checked the ground. No hazards, but he kept a grip on her since she was wearing some kind of fancy footwear that could lead to a sprained ankle. "So am I, but why didn't you contact Dallas?"

"I was about ready to do that when I saw your lights."

"How'd it go with him?" A flash of her calf told him she'd worn a skirt, or maybe even a dress.

"We'll discuss it in the warm cab."

"Touché." He steadied her on the short walk to his truck, handed her in and shut the door. The light from the cab had given him a pretty good view of her face. She still had a little bit of lipstick on. If Dallas had kissed her, and kissed her right, that wouldn't be the case.

Hurrying around the front of the truck, he climbed in and shoved his gloves in the pocket of his jacket before he shut the door and buckled up. The radio was playing Rascal Flatts' *I'll Be There.* Of course it was. It had been that kind of day. And night, evidently.

She gestured toward the dash. "Appropriate tune."

"Guess so." He glanced at her and tamped down a surge of lust. The effects of that dance still lingered. "Seems like the best option is driving you back to town."

"I don't want you to have to do that. Plus I need to deal with my truck and if I'm in town—"

"Jeremiah will tow it for you in the morning. You don't have to be here. He can stop by and pick up the keys from you."

"That still puts you out, having to drive all the way to town and then come home again."

"Not a problem. I'm assuming you don't want me to take you back to Dallas's place."

"God, no."

"That bad, huh?" It made him happier than it should.

"It wasn't bad at all. We agreed we're destined to be friends and nothing more. We have no chemistry and we both admitted it."

"I'll buy that you're not attracted to him, but I can't believe he's not attracted to you. Like I said, I saw his face last night. That boy was dazzled."

"At first, maybe. He might have been a little intimidated, but it wore off fast the longer we talked. He likes me. He admires me. But he never once had that gleam in his eye, the one that says he's thinking of me naked."

"Maybe he sensed you weren't into him so he controlled his response." Clint had that routine down pat.

"He wasn't doing that. But if you don't believe me, ask him yourself."

"No, thanks. I'll have to take your word for it." He put the truck in reverse and backed up a few feet so he could make a U-turn. "Looks like I'm taking you back to town."

"I have another idea."

He put on the brakes. Was it the same one he'd had all along? The really bad idea that sounded better and better the longer they sat in this cozy cab? His groin tightened. "What's that?"

"Would your mom be willing to put me up? That way you wouldn't have to make that drive to town and back."

Oh. He deflated, both mentally and physically. "Normally, she'd be happy to." How to explain it without revealing the family secret? "The thing is, she's working on... an important project and Rance told me tonight she's hit a snag. When that happens, we all know to stay away until she works through it."

"What sort of project?"

He dragged out one of the explanations the family had concocted years ago. He hadn't had to use it in awhile, so it didn't come naturally. "She...um...does some online stuff. For a big company. Complicated stuff. With deadlines." He sounded like a seven-year-old explaining what Mommy did for a living.

"You know, I always suspected she had something like that going on. She doesn't talk about it, though."

"She doesn't want to bore people."

"I'm sure she wouldn't, but clearly staying with her isn't an option."

"I'll just drive you to town. Happy to do it." He let up on the brakes and turned the wheel.

"Or I could stay with you."

He tromped on the brakes. "Meaning what?"

"I could stay at your place."

Turning, he looked at her, his pulse going like crazy. "You'll have to be more specific. I can't speak for you, but spending the night in the same house and not doing anything would be torture for me. I'm not signing on for that duty."

"What if we stayed in the same house and did something?"

He stared at her as the blood rushed in his ears. "Are you sure? Because we said—"

"I know what we said." She took a shaky breath. "But this situation gives us a chance to find out if having sex compromises our relationship at work. And the beauty of it is that nobody has to know except us."

"You're forgetting your truck is stranded on the side of the road. That'll alert folks that something's going on."

"Not if you take me back early enough that no one sees you. It'll be the same as if you took me back right now, except we'd have those few hours to—"

"Someone will find out." But what if they didn't?

"They won't if you can keep a secret."

He gripped the wheel because he'd started to shake. "I can keep a secret, but I need more info. Let's say we get away with spending a few hours alone and we enjoy that time." Ha. *Enjoy* didn't even begin to cover it. "Then what?"

"We'll evaluate our working relationship for the next few days. If it's not affected by what happens tonight, great. But if it is..."

"It won't be. I'll see to it."

"I hope it won't, either. We're taking a risk, though." She glanced at him. "I think it's worth taking, but if you—"

"I'm in." He spun the tires as he peeled out.

"Better slow down. You can't go roaring past Dallas's place. He might hear you, wonder who's driving like a maniac and step outside to look."

"Right." He eased up on the gas and remembered to breathe. If only he could shift his heart into a lower gear, but it was off to the races.

"Oh, damn. I promised him I'd text when I'm home safe."

"When did you leave?"

"Not that long ago. If I do it now he'll think I drove ninety miles an hour to make it to town that fast."

"My house is right up ahead. Once we get inside, I promise I won't remember that texting chore, and if I'm doing my job, you won't, either."

"I'll set the alarm on my phone." She pulled it out of her purse.

"That's gonna be romantic, having an alarm go off in the middle of the action."

"Do you have a better idea? If I don't text him, he'll wonder if something happened to me, and then he might—"

"Oh, you have to text him. When can you do it so he'll believe your story?"

"About fifteen minutes from now."

"Then here's the plan. When we get inside, you wait in the living room until it's time. I'll go to my bedroom and stay there. When you've texted him, come on back."

"I guess that'll work. Although it'll feel weird hanging out in your living room while you're—"

"You can take off your clothes."

"In your *living room*?"

"Not a soul will see you. I'll take mine off, too. It'll save time."

She began to giggle. "Naked in separate rooms. Hey, when I've texted him, I'll call out to you and we can run to meet each other in the hallway."

"Not unless you want to do it in the hallway."

"I want to do it in that beautiful bed you made. But you have to admit this is nutty."

"You're the one who promised to text him. I still say he's into you. Wanting confirmation that you made it home safely is a dead giveaway. By the way, what sort of lie are you planning to tell him?"

"I'll just say my truck broke down and you drove me home. He doesn't have to know I'm at your house instead of mine. I've been here before. It's not a lie."

"You must be a hell of a lawyer."

"I am."

"And we're here." Pulling into his usual spot, he switched off the engine. "Considering the plan, I won't bother to turn on lights like I did last night. The porch light filters in there. Should be enough." He unlatched his seatbelt. Still shaking. And hot. It was a wonder he wasn't steaming up the cab. Oh, wait. He was. "I'll come around and get you."

"No, don't. I might grab you."

"I might grab you right back."

"Go on inside. I'll let myself in and handle this blasted texting thing."

He started to open his door and paused. "What if he texts you back? What if he wants to have a late night conversation?"

"I'll tell him I'm safe and I'm going straight to bed."

He sucked in a breath. "Like I said, hell of a lawyer. See you soon." He climbed out while he could still walk. This would be a long damn fifteen minutes. Now it was more like ten, but that was about nine more than he'd prefer.

Moving quickly, he clattered up the steps and opened the door as she exited the truck. He left the door slightly ajar and lengthened his stride so he'd be inside his bedroom with the door shut before she came in.

And she began to strip. Probably shouldn't have suggested that maneuver. The visual would torment him throughout this enforced separation. His coordination was shot. Switching on the bedside lamps and adjusting the dimmer to achieve a mellow glow took way longer than it should have.

Folding back the covers, he fluffed the pillows. Then he pounded them a few times to release some tension. Didn't do much good. Hey, speaking of expiration dates....

He checked the nightstand drawer. His stash was still viable, but he hadn't touched it in two years. Sort of embarrassing to admit he'd been celibate for such an extended period. Because of that, he might not be the long-lasting stud he wanted to be, at least not the first time. If she was as keyed up as he was, she might not care.

He shucked off his clothes, carefully freeing his extremely stiff buddy. Couldn't afford to damage that critical part of his anatomy. No doubt about what he was looking forward to, was there?

He wouldn't greet her like this. Not classy. Under the covers was a better plan. He left his clothes on one of the chairs by the wood stove. He'd need them again when he took her home.

That was a key part of the plan. They had to leave soon enough for him to sneak back home before anyone was the wiser. Although he'd resisted the idea of an alarm to remind her about the text, he'd better set one to keep them on schedule.

Not that he'd fall asleep. But he could definitely lose track of the hour. He set his phone alarm. Should he get in bed yet? How long had it been? He'd been too distracted to check the clock on the dash when she'd given her fifteen-minute estimate.

Did he have time to shave? He rubbed his chin. Should've thought of that sooner. It'd be bad enough to greet her with a woody. It'd be worse to present her with a woody and a face full of shaving cream.

To hell with it. Might as well give her a shout and get an update. When he opened the door a crack, his brain checked out. She strolled toward him, her voluptuous body backlit by the glow from the porch. The slice of light from the bedroom gave him a tantalizing glimpse of creamy skin. He threw open the door.

And lost what was left of his mind. She paused, her green eyes luminous, her breath coming in quick little gasps that made her perfect breasts tremble. He'd created this fantasy a million times. Damn it, if he was dreaming...

"Happy to see me?"

"You..." He paused to clear his throat. "You have no idea."

"Can I come in?"

"Please." He reached out. His hand miraculously steadied when she slipped her fingers through his. He tightened his grip. Not a dream. This was real. And right. He'd never been so sure of anything in his life.

Holding her gaze, he drew her into his arms. Contact. Skin to incredibly soft, warm skin. He dragged in a breath. Shivered in anticipation.

"Is it like you imagined?"

"Better." He let go of her hand so he could tuck her in closer. His heart hammered as his needy cock pressed against her belly. "Way better."

Winding her arms around his neck, she nestled against him and tipped her face up to his. "I like this."

"Me, too." He dipped his head, his mouth hovering over hers. "Fair warning, once I kiss you, all hell's liable to break loose."

"I'm counting on it."

"Then here goes."

_15_

Tyra's body pulsed with eagerness as Clint's mouth drew closer to hers. When he'd opened the door, she'd almost tackled him. One glance at his muscled body, aroused and handsomely endowed, had sent moisture rushing to her lady parts.

But instead of launching herself into his arms, she'd stood still and allowed the delicious tension between them to reach a fever pitch. So worth it. Held tight against his broad chest, she absorbed the rapid drum of his heart and breathed in the sharp, heady scent of a hot-blooded male.

He touched down gently at first. Then, with a groan, he took full possession of her mouth with a firm thrust of his tongue. Spreading his fingers over her tush, he picked her up, his cock pressing hard against her belly as he carried her to his bed.

He laid her on the cool sheets and followed her down, his kiss moving from her mouth to her throat to the tips of her breasts. Lingering there, he slipped his hand between her damp thighs. His breath hitched. "Ah, Tyra."

She gulped as he began to caress her. "Now you know all my secrets."

"Not all." He raised his head and met her gaze. "Only that you want this."

Her breathing went all wonky, making it hard to talk. "You... knew that... before." Her core tightened as his attention became more focused. Was she really this close to a climax? Yes, she was.

"I didn't know for sure. Guys are an open book. But a woman? You don't know until she lets you touch her right...here." He brushed his thumb lazily over her trigger point, then applied more pressure.

She gasped. "Clint..."

"And here." He pushed his fingers deep.

She erupted, arching off the bed and crying out as the waves of her orgasm crashed over her again and...oh, yes...again. He continued to stroke her, prolonging the exquisite pleasure until she sank back to the mattress, breathing hard. "So...lovely."

"Yes, you are." Sliding his hand free, he shifted his position. His lightly furred chest grazed her taut nipples as he looked into her eyes. "I'm crazy about you, Tyra.""

"I'm getting that." The warmth in those blue eyes gave her the shivers. A good kind of shivers.

"I'm about to give you more proof. But first I have to suit up." Reaching across to the nightstand, he pulled out the drawer and snagged a foil package.

"That sounds promising."

"Don't be too excited. I'll probably last about six seconds." Sitting back on his heels, he ripped the package open. "Please forgive me."

"Are you kidding?" She shoved a pillow under her head for a better view as he rolled on the condom. "That's quite a gift you're wrapping. No apologies necessary."

"Kind of you to say." He changed positions, moving over her and bracing his weight on his forearms. The tip of his sheathed cock nudged the spot he'd recently made very happy. "I want it to be great for you, too, but after dreaming of this moment for years…"

"Years?"

"Afraid so."

"Then what the heck are you waiting for?" She'd been eager to grab his tempting buns ever since she'd managed to catch a glimpse during phase one. Now was the time. She gave him a good squeeze, which resulted in a sharp inhale on his part. "Go for it, cowboy."

"Yes, ma'am." He plunged in and went very still.

On her side of the action, nothing was still. Her pleasure palace was throwing a party and he was so invited. Except he hadn't moved. At all. "Something wrong?"

"No." His voice was tight, like he might be clenching his jaw.

She looked up and sure enough, his eyes were squeezed shut and his jaw was rigid, almost as rigid as the part of his body currently residing inside hers. "Are you sure you're okay, because—"

"I'm fine." Clearly he was gritting his teeth.

"I'm fine, too. I'm even—"

"I can feel you."

"I can feel you, too. You just twitched."

"Tyra..." He muttered a swear word and began to move, thrusting fast.

A little friction melded with their tight connection was all she needed. She came, shouting her praise for an orgasm twice as powerful as the first one he'd given her. With an impressive bellow, he shoved deep, his body shuddering against hers as he gulped for air.

As her breathing returned to normal, he continued to tremble in the aftermath. Stroking his back, she lay quietly and savored the connection. And not just the obvious physical one, although that was pretty darned great. But sharing this moment of surrender had created the warmth of an emotional bond.

Gradually his tremors ceased and she opened her eyes to peek up at him.

He was looking back, his expression slightly dazed, but also...triumphant? Slowly the corners of his mouth turned up. "You came."

"Yes, I did. And it was spectacular."

"Really? Spectacular?" The gleam of pride in his eyes grew brighter.

"Uh-oh. Now you're going to get a swelled head."

"As a matter of fact, I think I am. It seems all I had to do was—"

"Maybe so."

"No maybe about it. You were on the brink before I moved."

"Is that a big deal? You're acting like it's a big deal."

"I've never been with someone who was on fire from the get-go." He hesitated. "Okay, so it could be you and not me, now that I think about it. Maybe it's always that way with you. It's not that I'm so special. You're—"

"At the risk of creating a monster, I'll confess that I've never had that happen before. It's a first."

He grinned. "Excellent. That makes me very happy."

"Might be a one-time thing."

"Then we'll just have to test that, won't we?"

Her body started to hum. "I suppose we will."

"Don't go away." He leaned down, his kiss gentle, sweet. "Be right back." He left the bed.

Whew. So far this episode was one for the record books. She stretched her arms over her head and touched the smooth wood of the headboard. Maybe that was the magic in the equation. Turning over, she propped her chin on her hands and gazed at the intricate carving.

This close, she noticed that he'd used more than one piece. Made sense. He'd need a giant sequoia to create something this massive from one plank. Instead he'd matched the grain so well that the seams barely showed.

"That headboard has never looked better than it does right now. You add the finishing touch."

She rolled to her side as he approached. "It's magnificent." So was he. Not every man looked better without clothes than with them, but he certainly did. "How long did it take you?"

"Too long." He climbed into bed and lay facing her. "I finished soon after you moved back to town."

It took a moment for that to sink in. "Then you haven't had…"

"A woman in this bed since I made it? No, I haven't. My family's been over to look at it. They didn't think I'd ever finish, so we had to have a party when I was finally done."

She picked up his left hand and examined it. He had a white scar under his thumb, another on his middle finger and a newly healed reddish-pink slash on his wrist. "Battle scars?"

"Pure clumsiness."

"A clumsy man couldn't have made this headboard." She kissed each place where he'd cut himself and in the process found two more scars.

"Distracted, then."

"I've never known a wood carver."

"Well now you do." He drew his hand away and slipped it around her waist. "Intimately."

She snuggled closer. He was extremely good at snuggling. "I can't imagine the patience it must take for such a large project."

"Sometimes I get frustrated that I'm not making more progress, like with my mom's floor lamp, but in the end, it's worth taking the time to get it right."

"Clearly it is." She traced the line of his beard-roughened jaw. "Where's your wood shop?"

"Behind the house."

"And that's where you're working on your mom's lamp?"

"Yes, ma'am." Working his way up her back, he gave her a slow massage.

"I'd love to see—"

"Sure thing." Cupping the back of her head, he leaned over and nibbled on her mouth. "Another time. When we're dressed and the clock's not ticking. I set an alarm, by the way."

"So did I."

He drew back to gaze at her. "You did? Where's your phone?"

"At the end of the hall. Volume's on high."

"That's funny. I should have known."

"What time is it, now?"

"Time to think about something else." He cupped her breast, his fingers flexing as he teased her nipple with his thumb. "We've got dual alarms. Let's pretend we have all the time in the world. Until we don't."

"I like that idea." His caress was having a predictable effect. "I also like the way you fondle me."

"Can't help myself. I love touching you."

"Same here." She laid her palm over his heart. "You have sexy chest hair."

"Do I?"

"Oh, yeah. That's one of the reasons the bidding went so high when you wore nothing but turnout pants and suspenders during the bachelor auction."

"And here I thought it was my dancing."

"That, too, but your manly chest created a lot of excitement."

"Just so you like it."

"I do." She moved her hand lower. "Your abs are nice, too. You must work out."

"Some."

"Of course my personal favorite is this." She wrapped her fingers around his thick cock. "I think we're ready to run another test." She squeezed gently.

His breath caught. "You just read my mind."

"So it's true that guys think with their—"

"Yes, ma'am. And the more you stimulate that brain, the weaker the other one gets. My IQ just dropped fifty points."

"Maybe you should get one of those little raincoats."

"Believe I will while I still have the sense to do it." Reaching behind him, he fumbled with the drawer and eventually got his hand on a foil packet.

"Will you let me put it on?"

"Be my guest." He gave it to her.

"How about lying on your back? We can find out what happens when I'm in charge."

"Probably a good idea." His voice was husky as he stretched out beside her. "Since I can barely remember my own name."

She straddled his muscular thighs and ripped open the foil. "Can you remember mine?"

"I think it starts with a T."

"You're ridiculous."

"And you're the most beautiful woman who's ever rolled a condom on my pride and joy. Whoever you are."

She started giggling. "I don't think I've ever been laughing and turned on at the same time."

"Welcome to my world."

"All I can say is—" She rolled the condom in place. "By the time I'm finished with you, mine will be the only name you'll remember."

"That I believe."

Leaning forward, she braced her palms on his chest as she scooted into position. "You're breathing kinda fast, cowboy."

"That's your fault. I was cool and collected until you started in on me, playing with my privates, flashing your sexy body at me."

"Am I too much for you?"

"Probably." He grasped her hips. "Let's find out."

"Remember this is my show."

"Hey, you grabbed my butt last time. Turnabout's fair play."

"Okay, but let me lead."

"Yes, ma'am. That is your name, right? Ma'am?"

"Shush." She slowly lowered her hips, taking him in gradually.

He didn't say a word. He just groaned. And gulped in air.

Ah, this was glorious. As good as the first time. Better, even, with anticipation sending signals to her already vibrating core. She was panting a little, too. Almost there... done. Full immersion. She closed her eyes and reveled in the sensations spiraling out from their intimate connection.

"Can you come?"

His low, sexy voice sent shivers up her spine. "I'm holding off. Can you?"

"Always."

She checked to see how he was doing.

Instead of squeezing his eyes shut, he'd focused his gaze on her chest.

She leaned toward him. "Like what you see?"

"Uh-huh." He let go of her hips and shoved two pillows behind his head. "Closer, please."

She gripped his shoulders and gave him what he wanted. What she wanted.

Cupping a breast in each hand, he guided her nipple into his mouth, drew it in and stroked with his tongue as he gently sucked.

The rhythmic caress lit a fuse that traveled straight to the center of her body. The clench of an impending climax made her gasp.

He drew back, his eyes darkened to navy. "Go for it."

With a wild cry, she rode him, coming fast and hard. So did he. At the end he grabbed her hips and held her in place as he thrust upward, his cock pulsing deep within her.

Collapsing on his sweaty chest, she laid her cheek over his rapidly beating heart. Finally she was able to take a long, deep breath. "Will we ever…have…slow sex?"

He wrapped his arms around her and heaved a sigh. "Maybe sometime. But not tonight."

<u>16</u>

Clint had been right. Slow sex wasn't in the cards. He and Tyra made love twice more before their alarms chimed. Neither of those times could be described as slow sex. He wouldn't mind trying for that, but evidently they'd bottled up their cravings for too long to take a leisurely approach to mutual satisfaction.

And now their interlude was almost over. Although he'd told her to forget about the clock, he wasn't able to do it. Setting an alarm always heightened his sense of time, and *Amarillo by Morning* would come on any minute.

Because of that, he held her close but didn't try to start anything. She'd snuggled against him but wasn't making overtures, either. As if she understood.

And there it was, George Strait announcing the end of this adventure.

"That's your alarm."

"Yes, it is." He'd left his phone on the table by the wood stove, which meant he had to leave the bed to turn it off. He'd planned it that way.

"We need to get up."

"In case you haven't noticed, I am up."

Her low sexy laugh added fuel to the fire. She wiggled free and gave him a gentle shove. "Get out of here, cowboy, before I tackle you."

"Is that a promise?"

"Yes, and then we'll be late and the whole program falls apart."

With a sigh of resignation, he threw back the covers and swung his feet to the floor. "Damn, it's cold out here."

"That should take care of your problem."

He stood. "It will, smarty-pants." Walking over to the table, he picked up his phone and silenced George. A fire in the stove would be nice right now. Wouldn't be happening.

Then her alarm chimed from the far end of the hall.

"And there's mine." She sat up in bed, her fiery hair tousled and her green eyes sparkling with interest as she surveyed his naked self.

If he didn't move immediately, he'd end up back in that bed. "I'll fetch your clothes and your phone."

"Thank you. I'll freshen up in the bathroom."

He skedaddled out of there, resisting the urge to watch her climb out of bed. Picking up her phone on the way into the living room, he glanced at the screen. Another text from Dallas. A pang of guilt hit his gut. She was convinced the lack of chemistry was mutual, but he'd just torpedoed any chance that firefighter had.

She'd laid her clothes and her coat over the back of the couch. Her fancy footwear sat neatly on the floor in front of it. Technically they were boots but the skinny four-inch heel disqualified them as far as he was concerned. And the bling.

Her underwear lay on top of her dress. He picked up the silky underwire bra and skimpy panties. Although the living room was cold, too, the tactile pleasure of her undies got a rise out of him. Rolling them up, he shoved both into one of her boots. He laid her dress over his arm, scooped up the boots and headed back down the hall.

Maybe she wore sexy underwear all the time. But in his experience, most women, especially in the winter months, preferred cotton for everyday. They only pulled out seductive underthings when there was a chance someone else would be taking them off.

And damn it, he was glad that Dallas hadn't been the guy to do that. Neither had he, but next time—*whoa, dude. Might not be a next time.* With that depressing thought swirling in his head, he walked into the bedroom right as Tyra came out of the bathroom looking so beautiful it made his chest hurt.

"Thank you for bringing my stuff." She held out her hands. "I'll go put it on."

He gave her everything and she disappeared into the bathroom again. Why not dress out here? The obvious answer didn't improve his mood. She was already creating distance, preparing for later today at the Buffalo when they'd pretend this never happened. She didn't close the door, though. That was something.

He started putting on his clothes. As he was tucking his shirt into his jeans, the click of her high-heeled boots announced she was coming back. He glanced toward the bathroom door. The black knit material hugged her figure. He took a step forward, longing to gather her close. Caught himself. "Nice dress."

"Thanks. I hardly ever wear one these days." Her attention strayed to his fly as he zipped up his jeans.

It wasn't much of a tell, but he'd take it. "Ready?"

"Guess so." She glanced around the room and let out a sigh. "I hate to leave."

Then don't. "There's an alternative."

"I know." She met his gaze. "Don't think I haven't considered it. But we need to move carefully. A lot's at stake."

"Agreed." He put on his jacket. And his poker face. "Got your phone?"

"Right here." She held it up.

"Then let's go." He gestured toward the door and followed her out. She'd left her coat and purse hanging on the coat tree by the door. After helping her into the coat with brisk efficiency, he pocketed his keys, put on his hat and zipped his jacket. The blast of cold air when he opened the door slapped him in the face. A dose of reality.

But once they were on their way, cocooned in the toasty cab, ignoring Tyra's sensual pull was tough. The radio could sabotage him so he left it off. Conversation would help. What was a good neutral topic? "I'm glad it didn't snow during the night."

"Me, too."

So much for that. Silence reigned again. Her soft breathing teased him with memories of her silky skin, her warm caress, her body entwined with his after they'd made love. Every time she shifted in the seat, he tensed.

Then she came to the rescue. "How was the band last night?"

Thank you. "It was good. The Thursday night crowd liked them. Folks danced, made some requests. Jim made an announcement before the first set that they were filling in for the Trucks, who would be back soon. The Friday night crowd will be more of a test, but it looks like you found us a solid replacement."

"Excellent. Maybe I'll hang around for a little while tonight so I can see for myself."

"I'd like that." The words slipped out. "Don't worry. I won't ask you to dance."

"Probably not a good idea."

"The fact is, I enjoy your company."

"I enjoy yours. I always have. Those summers we waited tables together were fun."

"Yes, ma'am." *Fun* didn't quite cover it. He'd cherished every minute.

"I'd love to dance with you again, but I suppose we should hold off until we see how everything's going."

"Definitely."

"You're a great dancer. Did you pick that up on your own?"

"Mom taught all of us. Everybody liked it."

"Even Cheyenne?"

"Oh, yeah. He's fine with a partner. It was just that solo performance that threw him for a loop."

"Then everyone in your family can dance as well as you?"

"More or less. Evidently I inherited a little of my dad's talent. Mom says he's the best dance partner she's ever had."

"That skill must have come in handy as an actor."

"It has. That's another thing he loves about the Buffalo, dancing to a live country band. For that matter, so do I." Especially with her. "You're good at it, too."

"I should be. I've taken lessons since I was four."

"Seriously?"

"I wanted to be a ballerina."

"No, kidding."

"I held onto that dream until puberty, and after that it was a non-starter."

"Why?"

"I didn't fit the body type. A professional ballerina needs to be thin and flat-chested."

"Oh. I suppose they do." And she certainly wasn't flat-chested. His hands flexed on the steering wheel as he forced himself away from that subject. "Were you upset?"

"At first I was. I switched to jazz and tap, but they didn't thrill me like ballet. Then I learned about the wildlife conservation movement, and the more I got into it, the less I mourned my ballet career."

"With all that training it's obvious why you were such a great cheerleader."

"I ate that up with a spoon. Dancing with you at the Buffalo yesterday reminded me of how much I miss it."

"Why don't I ever see you out on the floor?"

"Nobody asks. I could approach the single guys who show up, but as the owner of the place, that feels weird. I'll bet they hesitate to ask me for the same reason."

"What about line dancing?"

"I've tried that a few times. Inevitably I get too fancy and attract more attention than I meant to. I don't want to be the star. That was fine when I led the cheer squad, but—"

"It would be fine, now."

"I don't agree. As the owner of—"

"I never pictured you hiding your light under a bushel, but I swear that's what it sounds like you're doing."

"No, I'm not. It just seems inappropriate for the owner of the place to put on a show."

"If the owner is you, there's nothing inappropriate about it. You're the one who told me you have a reputation in town as a powerhouse. Why worry about attracting too much attention for doing something you're very good at?"

"Did you ever see my dad out there line dancing with the customers?"

"No, but it doesn't matter. He did things his way and you're free to do things your way." He pulled up in front of her house and turned to her. "I'm serious about this. You're a wonderful dancer and if I didn't think it would get us both into trouble, I'd ask you."

"Well, I'm not inviting customers to dance with me."

"I can kind of understand that. And full disclosure, after what we just shared, I'm not eager for some other guy to put his arms around you. Line dancing is the perfect alternative, though. I hope you—"

"I'll give it some thought." She reached for the door handle.

He shut off the engine. "Hang on. I'll get the—"

"Better not." She touched his arm. "Stay where you are. If you help me out, you'll want to walk me to the door. If you walk me to the door, I'll want to kiss you. If I kiss you—"

"We'll be inside your bedroom before we know it." He sighed. "But I just want to say that this was—"

"Yes, it was."

"You'll need a ride to work in the morning. I'll come by and get you."

"No need. I'll text Vern in the morning. He goes right by here." She squeezed his arm and opened the door. "I'll see you at the Buffalo." Climbing out quickly, she closed the door and hurried up the walk.

He sucked in a breath when her boot heel caught on a chunk of ice, but she righted herself and made it the rest of the way without incident. He needn't have worried about those spiky-heeled boots tripping her up. She'd spent years balanced on her toes.

Once she was inside she flicked the porch light on and off. He turned the key and drove away from her house.

Funny how life worked out. The luscious curves he'd paid homage to tonight had sidelined her promising ballet career. If she'd realized that dream, her drive and self-discipline could have taken her to the top of the heap, putting her out of his reach for good.

Instead, she was back in Wagon Train and he'd been granted a few hours of pure heaven with the love of his life. He wanted more. What idiot wouldn't? But if that was all he'd ever have, he'd take it and be grateful.

17

Clint managed to grab some sleep after he got home and might have squeezed in some more shuteye except he'd left his phone on the nightstand. The familiar ring jerked him out of a hot dream about Tyra. He picked up his phone and tapped the screen. "Dad?"

"Hey, there, son. I'm in Missoula in the process of renting a car. I jerry-rigged this trip and wasn't sure whether it would come together. I barely made the last connection but here I am. Any chance I can bunk with you for a few nights?"

"Of course! How long can you stay?"

"I've booked a red-eye for Monday night, which only gives us three and a half days but I decided to take advantage of a break between projects. The last one wrapped up on Wednesday and the new one starts shooting next week."

"Three and a half days is better than nothing. Cheyenne will be excited. Have you called him?"

"Started with you since I didn't know his schedule and I also figured I'd be staying with you since I'm not about to barge in on the newlyweds.

But if you have a live-in lady friend I don't know about, then I'll—"

"I don't, and the guest room is yours. Can't wait to see you. Cheyenne's on duty through Sunday morning, but he might be able to switch with someone."

"If not, at least I'll get to see him for a couple of days. I knew I was taking a chance on you guys being available. You must have way more responsibilities at the Buffalo than you did last time I was there."

"I do, but my schedule's flexible. My boss is great." And that comment had a new meaning since last night's episode.

"That's still Tyra, I hope?"

"Yep."

"Frank let me know she'd agreed to take over, but I haven't heard from him recently. She's happy being back in Wagon Train?"

"Seems to be. Anyway, I'm not due at the Buffalo until ten. If you can get here before nine-thirty, we can—"

"Are you kidding? I'll be there in forty-five minutes. We'll have some time to catch up."

The trip normally took an hour, but speed limits had never made sense to Nick Reynolds. After he'd lived in other parts of the world, they made even less. "Take it easy, Dad."

His father just laughed. "See you in forty-five minutes."

Forty minutes later, Clint had showered, shaved, made up the guest bed and straightened up the house. Fortunately he kept it fairly neat.

The coffee pot was burbling when his dad pulled up outside and honked the horn. Clint didn't bother putting on a jacket as he headed out the door and down the steps. He grinned when his father levered himself out of the low-slung seat of a yellow Corvette. "Nice ride, Dad."

"Can you believe some dude changed his mind about renting this beauty? They gave me a smokin' deal, so why not?"

"Because it's winter in Montana? You'd better pray we don't get a blizzard."

"We won't. My luck's running this weekend. I can feel it."

"I'm sure it is." Clint hugged his father, who gave him a bone-crushing embrace in return.

"So good to see you, son." His voice was husky. Stepping back, he smiled, his gaze warm. "Bad enough that I had to miss Cheyenne's wedding, but now that he and Kendall are expecting a baby girl, I had to come. Can you believe it? I'm gonna be a grandpa!"

"Sorry, but you don't look like one." Tanned, fit, wearing a black turtleneck, jeans and a leather jacket, he could pass for a man twenty years younger. "Not a gray hair on your head."

His dad chuckled. "George Clooney can get away with it. I can't."

"You look great. You always do."

"All part of the game." He patted his flat stomach. "Hey, I see smoke coming from your chimney and I smell coffee. I'll grab my carryon so we can move this reunion party into your cozy cabin."

"Want some breakfast?"

"If you're cooking, I'm eating." He took a small suitcase from the passenger seat and followed Clint into the house. "I admire your mother's determination to make all you kids self-sufficient."

"Marybeth and Buck had a lot to do with that, too."

"True, and they're both terrific, but Desiree set the tone. Incredible woman." He lifted the suitcase. "I'll tuck my stuff away and splash some cold water on my face. Be with you in a minute."

"I'll wrangle up some food. Oh, and I texted Cheyenne. He'll let us know whether he can rearrange his schedule."

"I hope he can."

"Me, too." Clint made tracks for the kitchen. He'd learned to cook from his mom and Marybeth, but he'd learned to cook fast from Vern at the Buffalo. Consequently, two servings of scrambled eggs, bacon and toast were on the table by the time his dad walked into the kitchen.

"That's impressive, son."

"Have a seat." He brought over two mugs of black coffee. "Cheyenne texted back. He has to work today and tonight, but he got Saturday off."

"I'm sort of glad he can't come right over." His dad took a seat. "There's something I've been dying to tell you, but it needed to be in person."

"That sounds ominous." Clint sat down.

"No, nothing bad. I understand you're doing the buffalo's voice these days."

"Who told you?"

"Frank."

"Why would he tell you?" He stared at his father in confusion. Then the pieces fell into place. "You were the voice."

"Bingo."

_18_

The text from Clint only said _Running late. Dad's here._ Tyra had been jumpy ever since she'd arrived at nine. She'd planned to dive into the inventory stats Clint and Vern had given her. Getting a handle on how this year compared with last should be important enough to absorb her attention. It wasn't.

Now Clint was on his way, possibly with his father in tow, and she couldn't sit still. Popping into the kitchen, she bummed a warm yeast roll from Vern, who'd just taken the pan out of the oven.

He glanced at her. "Clint here yet?"

"No, he's running late."

Vern's bushy gray eyebrows rose. "He never runs late."

"His dad's in town."

"Ah. That explains it. He's on Nick Reynolds time."

"What?"

"That's his dad's name. Nick's a great guy, but he—"

"You know him?"

"Sure. He loves the Buffalo."

"I can't believe I've never met him."

"No reason to, really. He'd only show up once or twice a year. Never stayed long, but he always made a trip to the Buffalo. You were probably in school, or off at cheer camp. You were a busy girl. Is he coming in with Clint?"

"I don't know."

"I'll bet he is. Good thing I'm not out of pastrami. Nick loves the way I make my Reubens."

"Now I hope Clint does bring him."

"If he does, Nick will insist on coming in through the front door. He gets a kick out of that talking buffalo."

"Then maybe I'll go help Cecily with the setups." She finished the yeast roll and walked out to the dining room where her most experienced server, a petite blonde, was putting the finishing touches on the dining tables. Cecily was another Buffalo veteran who was worth her weight in gold. "Hey, Cecily, I just heard that Clint's dad is in town."

"Is he? It'll be good to see him. It's been a while."

"You know him, too?"

"All the old hands do. He loves this place. You haven't met him?"

"Amazingly, I haven't, but this might be the—"

"Oh, my goodness." Cecily glanced out the street-side windows and started laughing. "That's so Nick Reynolds."

"What?"

"Take a look. You don't often see a Corvette parked in front of the Buffalo. Dollars to donuts Nick's behind the wheel."

Tyra glanced out the closest window as two tall men unfolded themselves from the racy yellow sports car. Clint grabbed his hat from the dash and settled it on his head. The other guy, who didn't look much older than Clint, buttoned his leather jacket. "That's his dad?"

"Yes, ma'am. I guarantee he's had work done. And colors his hair. He's gotta be pushing sixty."

"He sure doesn't look the same age as my dad."

"That's show biz for ya."

Tyra backed away from the window. She'd rather not be caught gawking at Clint and his dad, although they were a fascinating pair who looked more like brothers than father and son.

They paused outside the entrance, heads together, clearly deep in a discussion about something. Then Clint's dad opened the door walked past the buffalo and grinned. "Epic. Back out a ways, son. I gotta hear that again."

Clint obliged and his father enjoyed another rendition of *Hey, there, daaarlin. Will yooouu be myyy Vaaalentiiine*?

His chuckle of delight startled Tyra. He sounded exactly like Clint.

"Hello, Tyra." He walked toward her, his hand outstretched. "I'm Nick Reynolds, Clint's dad."

"I know. I mean, it's great to meet you." He had Clint's firm grip and the same sparkle in his blue eyes. Spooky. "I can't believe I never have."

"Ships passing in the night." He turned toward Cecily. "Hey, there, girl. You're looking younger every time I see you."

She laughed. "You, too, Nick."

"I try." Then he made a slow spin to take in all the decorations. "Nice job, Tyra."

"I went a little overboard."

"No such thing. Listen, there's something Clint and I want to talk to you about. Could we go back to your office?"

"Of course." As they walked toward the hallway, she sent a questioning glance Clint's way.

He looked like a little kid with a secret. "It won't take long."

"Want me to bring you guys coffee?" Cecily called after them, clearly wanting to know what this was all about.

"Not yet, lovely lady," Nick said over his shoulder. "But I'd love some when we come back. And a piece of—"

"Chocolate cake. You've got it."

Tyra ushered the two men into the office. Clint offered his desk chair to his dad before moving to the door and quietly closing it. Then he propped his hips on the edge of the desk.

"What in the world's going on?" She gazed at them. "I can't imagine what—"

"There's a reason you've never met me," Nick said. "Your mom and dad made sure of it. You were a smart little girl and you would have figured out who I was in no time."

"And who are you?"

"The original voice of the buffalo."

She was momentarily stunned, but then it all made sense. "Of course you are. You're an actor. And Clint has your same voice, so with a little coaching—"

"A lot of coaching," Clint said. "Frank worked me over the coals before he was satisfied."

"I know," his father said. "He sent me the demos and we discussed it."

"I didn't know that."

"You weren't supposed to know. But Frank and I talked about it a month ago, when I was hoping to put together this trip, and we agreed that you both deserve the truth before we croak."

"What?" Clint swung to face his dad. "Is something wrong with you?"

"I have a million things wrong with me, but nothing life-threatening. Still, only Frank and I knew the origin, and what if some freak thing happens and we both go within days of each other, or one dies and the other has a stroke, or—"

"This is depressing, Dad. How about we say you and Frank finally decided Tyra and I were responsible enough to be in on the big secret."

She bristled. "I can't speak for you, but I've always been responsible enough."

"You probably were," Nick said. "But everyone in town is curious about the voice of the buffalo. The temptation to tell your friends would have been overwhelming when you were younger."

"I still say I would have resisted."

"She would have," Clint said.

"Thanks for that. And while we're on the subject, why was it so critical to keep this under wraps?"

"When Frank and I dreamed up the idea, I'd just joined the Screen Actors Guild. According to their rules, I couldn't do the voicing for free like I'd planned. I did it anyway because Frank couldn't afford that kind of money. But I was terrified of getting in trouble with SAG. So I made Frank swear it wouldn't come out."

"But I'm not a member of SAG," Clint said. "So now—"

"The secrecy is a big marketing advantage." Nick looked at her. "Agreed?"

"Agreed. It adds a layer of mystery. I always thought that was the reason for it. At this point, it still is." She studied Nick. "Then you were the guy who came to the house after I'd gone to bed."

"That was me."

"I heard your voice, but you kept it low. If you'd talked normally, I might have noticed that Clint's sounds like the mystery person I heard when I was a kid."

"Or not. You weren't looking for a connection. But now the mystery is solved. And you two probably have work to do, so if you'll excuse me, I'm gonna grab a slice of cake and a cup of coffee." He stood. "Then I'm outta here."

Clint got up, too. "But you're coming back here for dinner, right?"

"Wouldn't miss it."

Tyra left her chair and came around the desk. "I'm glad we finally met."

"It was time. I hear you might stay to check out the new band."

Interesting that Clint had mentioned that to his dad. "I was thinking about it. If you're having dinner here, then I'll plan on it."

"Great. Since Cheyenne's working, I'll see if Kendall might like to come. Maybe Desiree would like to, and some of the others for that matter. We could make a party of it."

"Fair warning, Dad. Last I heard, Mom's working through a snag in her latest project."

"I know how that goes. I'll text her instead of just showing up."

"Good idea."

"See you two tonight, then." He left, closing the door after him.

"Oh." Tyra started toward it. "We should—"

"In a minute." Clint took her by the shoulders. "We need to talk."

She looked up. "Talk?"

"Just talk." He let go of her. "Not that I wouldn't like to do more than talk, but we have a deal. You can step behind your chair if you're worried."

"That would be silly. What do we need to talk about?"

"Dad had a lot of questions about you and me working together."

"What kind of questions?"

"Like whether I still had a crush on you. I'd forgotten that I'd told him about it. He happened to visit right after you'd moved permanently to D.C. and I was pretty bummed."

And she'd been oblivious. "What did you say?"

"That I still had feelings for you but they were manageable. He asked how you felt about me, and I launched into the whole workplace romance boondoggle."

Her heart thumped faster. "I assume you didn't tell him about—"

"Last night? I would never do that. But he's like a sponge when it comes to emotions. He's liable to—"

"Is he staying with you?"

"Yes. He insisted on driving the Corvette to town and wanted me to ride with him so he could show me what she could do. It's a wonder we didn't get picked up."

"He still has a lot of kid in him, doesn't he?"

He smiled. "That's an understatement. And it's part of what makes him a good actor. Also why my mom refused to marry him."

"She turned down his proposal? Before or after she was pregnant with twins?"

"After. He thought for sure she'd say yes, but he didn't know my mom. She was excited about having us but she wasn't about to marry my dad when it was clear he'd be just another kid to care for."

"How does she feel about him, now?"

"Fine. If she's worked through the glitch on her project, she'll probably come to dinner. They get along well, but these days it's strictly platonic."

"That's fascinating."

"He's a likable guy."

"I can see that."

"I also think now that Cheyenne's married to Kendall and they have a baby on the way, he wants me to settle down with someone and have children, too, which is ironic because he's never achieved wedded bliss."

"Do you think he'll try to play matchmaker while he's here?"

"I wouldn't be surprised."

"When's he leaving?"

"Monday night."

"Considering that he'll be staying with you, I'd say we stand a good chance of foiling his efforts."

"That's my thought. I just wanted to warn you."

"Thanks."

"Tyra."

"Hm?"

"You keep drifting toward me. I've edged back twice."

"Oh!" She planted her feet. "Sorry. That's not very helpful, is it?"

"No, but it sure makes me happy. I'm glad you're staying for awhile tonight. Should be fun."

"That reminds me. Why did you tell your dad I was considering it?"

"The subject of dancing came up. I said you were very good at it but you didn't dance much now that you own the place. He plans on getting you out on the floor."

"You know, that would be perfect. He's a customer, but he's also a friend of the family. And obviously a good dancer since he's the one who took you to the next level. I'm glad your dad came to town."

"So am I."

"Clint." She stepped back.

"What?"

"You're drifting in my direction."

"It's your lipstick. I don't remember you wearing that color before. I was trying to get a better look."

"It's the same one I always wear."

"No, it's not. The other one was a peachy tone, but this one has more pink in it..."

Her breath caught. One more step and he'd be close enough to kiss her. "Get out of here, cowboy."

He drew back, desire flickering in his eyes. "Yes, ma'am." He opened the door and walked out.

Her hungry gaze followed him, focusing on those broad shoulders and firm butt as his long strides took him away from her.

<u>19</u>

From six o'clock on, the Buffalo was party central. Customers streamed in, including the bulk of Clint's family and even his mother. The bartender had only been on the job a few months and he was quickly overwhelmed. Clint considered asking Rance to help, but ended up going over there himself. Better to be busy.

His dad had asked Tyra to dance, and that move had turned out to be the nudge the young single guys needed. Every time Clint glanced in that direction, she was twirling around with someone new. Judging from her smile and flushed cheeks, she was having a blast.

Good. She didn't belong on the sidelines. She gleamed like the star she was, and when her hair caught the light, he'd swear it gave off sparks. If seeing her in the arms of other men made his gut clench, he needed to get over it. They were just kids.

"Clint, I need a little happy juice."

Startled out of his funk, he turned toward the gray-haired man leaning against the bar watching the dancers. Andy Hartmann published the town's weekly and last year had become Beau's father-in-law and the proud grandfather of little Maverick. At the moment, he didn't look his usual jovial self.

"What can I get you, Andy?"

"Two shots of JD on the rocks, please. Oh, and dancing lessons."

"Why?" Clint poured the drink and set it on a coaster. "I've seen you dance a bunch of times. You do just fine."

Andy faced him and picked up the glass. "Not fine enough to compete with Nick Reynolds." He took a hefty swallow.

"Ah." Until now, he'd zeroed in on Tyra. Scanning the kaleidoscope of whirling couples, he spotted his dad and mom putting on a show. And his mother was glowing with pleasure.

Andy and his mom had bonded during the emotional hours of Maverick's birth and being first-time grandparents had brought them even closer in the past year. Evidently Andy didn't appreciate Clint's flashy dad horning in on that cozy relationship. "This is the only time you'll have to deal with that. He's leaving town Monday night."

"So I heard. But folks will be dancing at your sister's birthday celebration at Rowdy Roost Tuesday night and my two-step won't stand up very well after this performance."

"Mom doesn't care. She values your friendship, not your dancing ability."

Andy sighed. "You're right. But she looks so happy. I wouldn't mind being good enough to put that expression on her face."

"Okay, I get it. She'd probably be touched if you made the effort to improve your game. And you'd both enjoy dancing together more."

"Exactly. I don't think we have any dance instructors in town. I'll have to drive up to Missoula, but that's actually better. It'll be more fun if I don't tell her I'm doing it."

"I could give you some lessons on the sly."

Andy's expression brightened. "Yeah? I love that idea. I'd be happy to pay—"

"Nope. It's free. If it doesn't work for you, then you can look for a pro. But I've learned most of what my dad's doing out there. I think I could pass it on to you."

"That sounds awesome."

"There's a lot going on right now, though, so we might have to wait until... you know what? My dad tends to sleep in and I guarantee he will tomorrow morning after that long plane ride and all the activity. If you can meet me here at eight, or earlier if you want, we could sneak in a lesson."

"That would be good timing for me. I put the paper to bed before coming over here tonight, so I'm relatively free. I could get over here by seven-thirty, but I hate to make you drive in that early."

"No worries. There's no reason for me to hang around the house while Dad's sleeping. He has a car."

Andy rolled his eyes. "Tell me about it."

Clint disguised his laughter with a cough. Poor Andy. "We might be able to do the same thing Sunday and Monday morning. Not Tuesday, though."

"I know. The birthday ride. I'm excited about that. Kendall's loaning me her dad's horse, Mayhem. She says the mare doesn't live up to her name."

"Nope. She's perfect for someone who doesn't ride a lot."

"I want to get better at that, too. Your mother's offered to give me pointers. I suppose she could do the same thing with dancing, but..."

"Surprising her will be more fun. Three lessons should give you some extra moves for Tuesday night."

"I'm in."

"I'll need to clear it with Tyra though, since we're using the Buffalo dance floor and sound system. Is it okay if she knows about it?"

"Of course."

"When you get a chance, would you ask her to come over here so I can let her know?"

"Will do."

"Better make it soon. It's slowed down, but by my calculations the band's about to take a break. Then we'll be swamped again."

"I'll get right on it." Andy laid money on the bar, picked up his drink and started to walk away. Then he turned back. "I got so wrapped up in my problem I forgot to ask what was bugging you."

"What do you mean?"

"When I started over here, you looked as out-of-sorts as I felt. Anything I can help with?"

"I doubt it."

"I'm a newspaper man, so I'm a good listener and I never reveal my sources."

"I appreciate the offer. I'll let you know if I need an ear."

"Do that." He walked back toward the McLintock section of the dining room.

Moments later, Tyra headed in his direction, her expression animated. "Andy said you wanted to see me about something."

"I do." He outlined the plan while greedily soaking up the glow she'd brought with her, the one her dance partners had been basking in. Lucky bastards.

She smiled. "What a wonderful idea. By all means, use the facility."

"Thanks. By the way, what's the story on your truck?"

"They had to order a part and it won't come in until the first of next week."

"Then I guess you'll have to catch a ride with Vern in the morning."

"He's not coming in until almost eleven because he did some advance prep this afternoon. But I haven't been that efficient today. I have some paperwork to catch up on."

"I could give you a ride, but it would be pretty early."

"It would be early and Andy might not appreciate having me here. Maybe I can find—"

"I could come get you after Andy's lesson. How does that sound?"

"More doable, but—"

"Nine?"

"All right. Thank you. By the way, how are you holding up?

"Clearly not as well as you are. Apparently my dad jumpstarted things by getting you out on the floor. You've barely had a chance to sit down."

"It's been great and I appreciate what he did. But now I'm beginning to fade."

"Doesn't show."

"Trust me, I can feel the warning signs. If I don't get out of here soon, I'll crash and burn. Aren't you about ready to call it a night?"

"I'll stick it out through the rush of orders during the break. After that, I'll work on Dad and see if I can get him out the door."

"Good."

"I'd offer to take you home, but we're in the Corvette—"

"No worries. I'm all set."

"Excellent."

"When this set's over, I'll leave with Beau and Jess. They need to pick up Maverick from Marybeth and Buck's house and they can drop me off on the way."

"Good plan."

She peered at him. "You sound a little down."

"Feeling sorry for myself, is all. I'm glad you had fun tonight. Selfishly, I wanted to be out there."

"I wish you could have been." She lowered her voice. "I did have fun dancing tonight, but it wasn't anything like dancing with you."

"Nice to hear."

"I don't know what will happen with us, but... there's something special going on." She held his gaze as the warmth in her eyes changed to something more potent.

His throat went dry. "Tyra, I—"

"I'll be ready at nine. Thanks again for offering to pick me up."

"Anytime." He gripped the beveled edge of the bar and resisted the urge to vault it and go after her. What then? Kiss her in front of everybody here? That would be the most stupid, selfish move he could make.

20

Clint took the wheel of the Corvette for the endless drive back to his cabin while his dad gave him romantic advice. After letting his dad know he'd be leaving early in the morning, he climbed into bed and dropped off immediately. His alarm roused him from a hot dream about Tyra — big surprise — and he hurried through his morning routine so he'd be on time for Andy's lesson.

The drive in with no distractions created the perfect space for his dad's words to come rushing back. *Tyra's action-oriented. She'll respond to a bold approach. Don't let fear slow you down. Doubt is your enemy. Think positive and go for it.*

His dad wasn't necessarily wrong. But his father also had crashed and burned many times using that strategy.

He parked in front of the Buffalo where Andy stood waiting for him with a mischievous grin. "Knowing this was coming improved the rest of my evening, what was left of it. I'd look at Nick Reynolds and say to myself *just you wait.*"

Clint laughed. "That's the spirit." He let Andy into the empty saloon. "It'll be chilly at first, but dancing will warm you up. Leave your coat and hat on a chair while I cue up the music." After ditching his coat and hat, he ducked behind the bar and turned on the sound system. Alan Jackson's *It's Five O'Clock Somewhere* should do the trick.

"Hey, I like that one."

"Me, too. Snappy but not too fast. Next lesson we'll pick up the pace." Clint walked out on the floor. "This'll take some imagination, but pretend I'm your lady friend. I'll take her part and coach you on yours."

Andy's eyes widened. "You're gonna dance with me?"

"Best way to show you and check out your technique. My brothers and I only had Mom as our partner when we first learned, so we had to switch roles all the time. That's how my dad taught me, too. He took the lady's part."

"I'll be damned. Okay, then." He put a tentative hand around Clint's waist. "You're a solid one."

"And you need a more assertive hold than that. Press your hand against the small of my back and keep the pressure firm, like you need to hold a hundred-dollar bill and not lose it. There, that's better. Get the sense of rhythm, then make your move."

Andy took a few small steps, not easy to follow.

"Like you mean it, Andy."

"Not sure I get it."

"Then we'll switch roles. You be the lady and I'll show you what I mean." He grabbed hold of Andy and took off, hauling him around the floor, guiding him this way and that, twirling him under his arm, not giving him a chance to hesitate.

Chuckles began spilling out of Andy and within minutes he was doubled over, impossible to dance with. His laughter was contagious and Clint gave up trying to be serious. Letting go of Andy, he began dancing alone, whirling around, hands over his head, hips keeping time with the music.

When the song ended, Andy applauded wildly and Clint responded with a deep bow.

"Oh, son." Andy pulled a handkerchief out of his back pocket, wiped his eyes and blew his nose. "I haven't had that much fun in years. Start that song again. I'm loosened up, now."

He was, too. He approached the dance with gusto. Yeah, he stepped all over the toes of Clint's boots, but they were old, worn today on purpose. They danced together the whole hour, until Andy sagged into a chair, breathing hard, his face shiny with sweat, his smile a mile wide.

"Have fun?"

"You know it. You wore me out, boy, but I'll be ready and eager to go again tomorrow. No wonder your mother loves dancing with someone who knows what the hell he's doing. So do I!" Cramming his hat on his head, he picked up his coat and stuck out his hand. "See you in the morning."

"Looking forward to it." Boy, wasn't that the truth. His life had become so damned complicated recently that this simple project was exactly what he needed. Dancing with Andy had worked the kinks out of his body and cleared fuzz from his brain.

He drove to Tyra's house in high spirits, eager to tell her all about Andy's first dance lesson. She'd get a kick out of hearing the details.

When she didn't answer the door right away, he pulled out his phone and called her. It went straight to voice mail. What the hell? He rang the doorbell again. Still no response.

Raising his fist, he was ready to pound on the door when the peaceful silence of the neighborhood finally made an impression. Banging on her door might alarm her neighbors. So would standing on the porch calling for her.

He had a key. Frank had given him one a few years ago so he could come in and record at will or run over to the house and fetch something for him when he was too busy to do it himself. He used it and walked straight in so he wouldn't look furtive to anyone watching.

Nothing stirred inside, either. No coffee had been brewed, no shower was running. "Tyra?" He called loud enough that she should be able to hear him even if she was upstairs. No answer.

Not wanting to shout, he started up the stairs. "Tyra? It's Clint. I'm here to—"

"Oh, my God."

Her soft cry of alarm brought him the rest of the way up the stairs. "Are you okay? Is something—"

"I overslept!" She ran out of her room wearing green plaid flannel pajamas and her hair going every which way. "I'm so sorry." She hurried toward him, her face pink with embarrassment.

"I'm just glad you're okay." And some parts of him were super glad. The soft flannel told him she wasn't wearing anything under her PJ top. Her pink cheeks made her eyes look mesmerizingly green. And her full lips were their natural shade, the same as they'd been after he'd made love to her for hours.

"I thought I'd set my alarm, but I was so tired and I... guess I didn't. You came all the way over here just to pick me up. I feel like an idiot for not setting the alarm and I..." She trailed off. "Are you mad at me? I can't tell for sure if you're upset or—"

"I'm not upset." Closing the short distance, he scooped her into his arms.

"Clint! I can guess what you're thinking, but we should—"

"Take advantage of a golden opportunity." He carried her back to her bedroom.

21

Tyra didn't resist when Clint laid her on the bed she'd just climbed out of, but when he tried to pull off her PJ bottoms she grabbed the elastic and held tight. "Wait a minute. This makes no sense."

"It makes perfect sense." Abandoning the tug-of-war, he hung his hat on her bedpost and shrugged out of his jacket. "I've been going crazy thinking about you, wanting to touch you, kiss you, love you." He toed off his boots and unbuttoned his shirt. "Judging from the look you gave me last night, you're in the same boat."

"What if I am?" He stripped off his shirt. Holy moly, he looked even more magnificent in the light of day. A wave of longing left her shivering with need.

"What if the two of us, each aching for the other one, have stirred up enough energy to create this situation, another gift from the Universe. Who are we to turn it down?" Tossing his shirt away, he unbuckled his belt.

Her attention focused on the belt... and the denim of his fly, stretched to the limit. "I don't have any—

"'Course not. I'd be surprised if you did." He unbuttoned, unzipped, and shoved his jeans and briefs over his hips. "That's not the only way to make love."

Swallowing the moisture pooled in her mouth, she let go of her waistband. "I know." Her nipples tightened and a hollow ache in her core messed with her breathing.

He shot her a quick look and smiled. "Yes, ma'am, that's the light in your eyes I was going for." After he stepped out of the jeans, he sat on the edge of the bed and pulled off his socks as nonchalantly as if he'd been undressing in front of her for years. "Don't need to do this, but I've never been fond of doing it with socks on." He dropped them on the floor and turned to her. "That does it."

Bracing a hand on either side of her, he maneuvered until he settled his hips between her thighs.

She gasped when his cock pressed down, sending a distinct message.

"That's it." He leaned over, his mouth hovering tantalizingly close to hers, his warm breath fanning her cheeks. "Pretend I'm deep inside you." He began to rock his hips. "Stroking you, loving you, making you come." His lips touched hers. He nibbled, licked and finally thrust his tongue inside to mimic the steady movement of his hips.

With a low groan, she wrapped her arms around him, surrendering to the delicious rhythm, the creak of the bed, the tension building within. Her thighs began to quiver.

He pushed firmly against the drenched flannel and lifted his mouth from hers to gulp for air. "Let go. Let go, Tyra."

Obeying his breathless command, she lifted her hips to tighten the connection.

"That's it." He moved faster. "That's it, sweetheart. *Come for me.*"

Fireworks! She cried out as they showered down on her again, and yet again in a sparkling array of sensual delight so intense that she grew dizzy.

"There you go." His soft murmur in her ear brought her gently down to earth.

She grinned. "Thank you."

"You're welcome." He nuzzled the side of her neck. "My pleasure."

"Speaking of that."

"No need." He slipped his hand under her PJ top to caress her breasts.

Arching her back and closing her eyes, she savored his warm, arousing touch. "Oh, you have a need. It's quite obvious."

"We'll take care of that tomorrow."

She stiffened. "Tomorrow?"

"Got another lesson with Andy."

"What's that got to do with... oh, you mean you could drive over here after." Was that a good idea?

"Yes, ma'am." He brushed his thumb across her nipple. "Next time I'll be better prepared." Pushing up her top, he changed position and used his hot mouth on her breasts until she began losing her mind...again.

By the time he slid his hand under her waistband she desperately wanted it there...yes...*there*. The man knew his business. Within seconds she fell headfirst into another shattering climax that left her breathing hard, limp and sated. And grateful. So grateful.

Her recovery was slow and languid. When she finally opened her eyes, she looked into blue eyes gleaming with smug satisfaction. She grinned. "Don't you look proud of yourself."

"As a matter of fact, I am."

"Well, guess what? Turnabout's fair play."

He shook his head. "Like I said, tomorrow I'll—"

"But tomorrow's a long time away. Roll over, buddy. I'm going to make you happy right now."

His gaze flickered. Clearly he was thinking about it. "I thought you had paperwork to catch up on."

"After the way this day started, I'll be supercharged when I get to the office."

"Does that mean you'll go along with my plan?"

"I'll go along with yours if you'll go along with mine. Roll over, cowboy."

He laughed and did it. "You drive a hard bargain, lady."

"Right backatcha, mister. I prefer hard bargains to soft ones." She sat up and surveyed the situation. Her core clenched. Of course it did. That beautiful sight made her want an experience she couldn't have at the moment. But thanks to Andy's dance lessons, tomorrow she'd—

"Do me a favor?"

She glanced up. "That's what I had in mind."

"Take off your top?"

"Sure." She pulled it over her head and threw it in the general direction of his head. It landed on his face. "How's that?"

"Counterproductive, smartass." He pulled it away. Then he brought it back and held it to his nose. "Smells great, though. I'll bet the bottoms do, too."

"Want those?"

"Yes."

Flopping to her back, she shimmied free of her bottoms and aimed for his face this time.

"Mm. Very nice."

"I know something that will be even nicer." She straddled his thighs, wrapped her fingers around the silken length of his manly equipment and squeezed.

He sucked in a breath.

"On edge, are you?"

"Yes, ma'am." His voice was tight.

"Glad I insisted on doing this?"

"Yes, ma'am." He gulped. "And if you'll just—"

"Happy to. I promise not to mess around, either." Leaning down, she took him in until the tip brushed the back of her throat. Then she applied strong suction and slowly raised her head.

His groan was loud, maybe even loud enough for the neighbors to hear. Oh, well. She was having too much fun to care. He only tolerated a few more of those moves before he came, yelling like crazy, even calling her name. For sure the neighbors heard *that*.

She stayed with him and swallowed the salty evidence of his climax while he continued to make a fair amount of noise. It was funny. And arousing. She tamped down that last reaction. No reason to be greedy when tomorrow morning was only twenty-four hours away.

After gently releasing him, she added a few swipes of her tongue as a bonus, which made his breath hitch each time she did it. Aftershocks were nice. He'd given them to her and returning the favor warmed her all over.

He moaned. "I'm wrecked."

She left her post and crawled up so she could see his face. His eyes were squeezed shut and he was still breathing like a marathoner at the end of a race. "Did I break you?"

"Maybe, but what a way to go." He opened his eyes.

"You do look slightly dazed."

"I'm a lot dazed." He paused to take in more air. "It's like I've been stripped naked."

"Um, you are naked." Should she be worried about his mental state? "Don't you remember taking off your—"

"I'm not talking about whether I'm wearing clothes or not. This is more like everything's gone."

"They're right down there, on the floor." She picked up a sock. "See?"

He grinned. "You're adorable."

"And you're starting to scare me. Maybe your brain is low on oxygen after all that yelling. How many fingers am I holding up?"

"Three fingers."

"No, *four*. Seriously, I wonder if shouting like that has—"

"The other one's a thumb. Three fingers and a thumb." He clasped her hand in both of his. "Let me explain. When you took control of this episode, I resisted letting you have it. You might *think* you were in control, but really, I would decide when I'd let go."

"I could be wrong, but you didn't sound like a man in control."

"I wasn't. Two seconds in I gave you the reins and just let it happen." He focused on her. "I've never done that. Not with anyone. So that's what I meant by feeling stripped naked. I held nothing back." He paused. "I guess I was pretty loud, huh?"

She smiled. "Very loud."

"And unlike me, you have close neighbors."

"I do."

"Sorry. I can't even promise I'll be quieter tomorrow morning." He reached up and trailed his finger down the side of her cheek. "Maybe you'll want to reconsider—"

"Nope."

"This isn't the way you expected things to go."

"Not at all. In fact, when your dad showed up I assumed his presence in your house would remove all temptation."

"Yet here we are."

"Uh-huh. But I'm leaving this bed and hitting the shower before I start kissing you again."

"Then go, because my resistance is shot."

She climbed out of bed and allowed herself one last glance. He certainly improved the look of her bedroom. "How about getting dressed while I'm in the shower?"

"Good idea." He sat up and swung his feet to the floor. "If we don't watch out, the Buffalo will open without me and I didn't ask anyone to cover. Want coffee? I probably have time to make you some."

"No, thanks." Okay, one more teensy peek. She sighed. Magnificent. "I'll get coffee at the Buffalo." She started toward the bathroom. "But if you'd please make me a PB&J, that would be awesome. I'll eat it on the way over there."

"Absolutely."

"Bread's in the breadbox, peanut butter and jam are in the door of the fridge, utensils in the drawer to the right of the dishwasher."

"Got it."

"Meet you by the front door in fifteen minutes." She walked into the bathroom and turned on the shower. Using all her shortcuts, she aimed for the fifteen-minute deadline she'd set for herself. She quickly put on jeans, boots and a silky black button-up shirt that matched her sensual mood. Pulling her hair into a ponytail, she added minimal makeup. Then she bounded down the stairs.

Clint stood waiting for her, his jacket on, a clear sandwich bag in one hand and his phone in the other. "That's impressive."

"Did you time me?"

He grinned. "Couldn't resist." He handed her the sandwich, tucked the phone in his jacket pocket and helped her on with her coat. "You're almost out of peanut butter."

"I have a backup." She grabbed her purse and her keys.

"I should have guessed." He followed her out the door and waited while she locked up.

"I still can't believe I overslept. That's so unlike me."

"I know. That's what had me worried." He followed her down the narrow walk to the curb, opened the passenger door and helped her in. "I almost left the motor running so the cab would stay warm. I didn't expect to come in. I thought you'd be ready and rush right out the door when I rang the bell."

"Good thing you didn't leave it running." But how had he gotten in? She took a bite of her sandwich, which he'd made with just the right proportion of peanut butter and jam. When he slid into the driver's seat, she put down the sandwich. "Great sandwich. Thank you."

"You're welcome."

"By the way, was my front door unlocked when you arrived? I was exhausted, but I don't usually forget to lock it."

He buckled his seat belt. "You didn't. I have a key."

"Oh! I guess that's a good thing."

He gave her a sizzling glance. "I'd call it a very good thing."

One hot look and she was squirming in the seat. With great effort she returned to the matter at hand. "But why do you have a key?"

"Your dad gave it to me a while ago and I honestly forgot it was on my keyring until this morning when I couldn't rouse you. I decided to use it instead of banging on the door or shouting out your name."

"Let me guess. You didn't want to make noise and alarm the neighbors."

He chuckled. "Ironic." He switched on the engine and adjusted the air vents to maximize the flow of heat. "I'll return the key if you'd rather I didn't have one."

"No, it's fine. Someone besides me should have one, and you're the logical person." And the one she trusted the most, come to think of it.

"Okay, then." He sounded pleased with her answer. "I checked my messages while you were getting ready. Cheyenne and Kendall are having my dad over for dinner and I'm invited, too. Rance is scheduled to handle the bar tonight, so that leaves me free to hang out with them for a little while."

"That should be wonderful."

"When I read the text, my first thought was to ask you to go with me, but that would be like hanging up a flashing neon sign."

"It would. Besides, you haven't seen your dad in a couple of years. The three of you deserve some time to be together. And Kendall can get better acquainted with the man who'll be her baby's grandfather."

"Although she knows him from the days when he visited more often. She was at our place more than she was at hers." He grinned. "Mostly following Cheyenne around like a devoted puppy, so she saw a lot of my dad back then."

"I'm sure you'll have a great time reminiscing. And if you don't mind dropping me off on your way back to the ranch, I'd appreciate it."

"Be glad to."

"And I do mean that you should drop me off. Pull up to the curb and I'll just get out."

"That's not how I—"

"I realize that goes against the grain with you, but for both our sakes, it makes the most sense. If you get my meaning."

He sighed. "I do. I won't get out."

"Thanks." She glanced over at him. "Did Cheyenne and Kendall say when their baby is due? If they did, I've forgotten."

"So have I. Too many things on my mind that night. I'll ask when I go to dinner."

"Just think, you'll be that baby's uncle."

"Yes, I will. It won't be the first time I became one. Maverick gave me that honor. But I have to say that knowing that Cheyenne will soon be a dad hits closer to home."

"Makes sense. You're twins. The same age."

"Not quite. I'm older by two minutes."

"Whoa. Two whole minutes. You're letting your little brother get ahead of you?"

"I can hear you giggling over there, but that's exactly what I've been thinking ever since I found out about the baby. Cheyenne, the quiet, unassuming one, will be a proud papa while I..." He blew out a breath. "That's juvenile. I'm a bigger man than that."

"Do you have a strong urge to have children?"

"I didn't think I did, but watching Beau with Maverick has got my mind going in that direction. He doesn't sugarcoat the experience. He's honest about the diapers, the teething, the responsibility. But he lights up when he talks about something new she's learned, or something funny she did. He says it's a tough job, but it's the best one he's ever had."

"Nice."

"How about you? I didn't realize you keep toys in one of your desk drawers until Beau told me."

"Yeah, I love the look on their faces when I pull something new out of my pocket."

"Is that all you need, then? You haven't considered having your own?"

"Oh, I have." Especially when the lyrics to *The Rest of Our Lives* ran through her head. "First I'd have to find the right guy to be their dad." Unfortunately, her current candidate came with big complications.

22

Clint admired the door prize certificates when Tyra brought them back from the *Sentinel*'s print shop. Later in the day, they had a three-way discussion with Vern regarding the inventory stats. Other than that, he concentrated on his job and she concentrated on hers. Very professional.

A little after five, he let her know he'd be leaving soon. Twenty minutes later they were back in his truck for the short trip to her house. He wished it could be longer.

He turned the key in the ignition. "Feel more caught up?"

"Definitely." She snapped the tongue into the seatbelt buckle and settled back. "Answered most of the emails. Returned a few phone calls. Got the inventory under control thanks to you and Vern. It was a good day."

"Are you still planning to go in tomorrow? I didn't think to ask that."

"I am, now."

"You don't have to come back with me in the morning." His body tightened. "You can just stay in bed."

"I'm probably being silly, but if I actually come in to work, then saying you came to pick me up is still true."

"Is it bothering you? Carrying on in secret like this?"

"A little. I made excuses to myself for Thursday night and this morning. Neither one was planned. Yes, we made the call to take advantage of the opportunity, so it's not like we didn't have a choice, but next time…"

His gut began to churn. "Want to call it off?"

"No."

"That's a relief. I've thought about it off and on all day."

"So have I."

"Must not have interfered with your work if you still got a lot done."

"If anything, it galvanized me."

"See?" He glanced over at her. "What if we're good for each other?"

"I think we can be. As long as everything goes smoothly."

"We'll just make sure it does."

"You can't guarantee that we'll always get along."

"Of course not. But I can guarantee that if you and I get crossways, I'll make sure the Buffalo's daily operation continues just fine."

"You say that, but you and I are the most important people at the Buffalo. When Tony and I broke up, we had two more weeks of working together before I left. It was hell. Snarled up the office real good. And we were just two cogs in a bigger machine."

"I'm guessing everyone in that office knew you had a romance going."

"They did, and that made it a hundred times worse when we broke up. The sympathetic looks, the whispers, our friends taking sides, even though they swore they weren't doing that."

"Your decision to keep this secret makes a lot more sense now."

"It's not foolproof. We could still screw up the whole shebang. But if I come to work with you, it gives us a plausible excuse for being together, especially since nobody knows about Andy's dance lessons."

"Good thing I'm an expert at keeping secrets." He pulled up in front of her house and put the truck in neutral. "I believe this is your stop."

Unfastening her seatbelt, she grabbed her purse from the floor and turned to him. "Have a wonderful time with your dad. Tell him I said hello."

"Okay."

"He thinks the world of you. Tomorrow morning I'll tell you all the nice things he said about you."

"Sorry, but I'll be way too busy to have that discussion."

She smiled. "See you at nine?"

"I'll be finished with Andy at eight-thirty."

"Then get here as soon as you can."

"That's more like it." He wanted a kiss but she'd laid out the parameters and he'd stick with them. "Have a good evening."

"Thanks." She opened her door. "Thought I might call my dad. Having yours here made me realize I haven't talked to mine recently."

"Tell him hi for me."

"I will. See you in the morning." She blew him a kiss and hopped out.

"No fair, Lindquist!"

Laughing, she shoved the door closed, gave him a wave and hurried toward the house.

He stayed until she was inside. Dragging in a breath, he put the truck in gear and drove away. If he hadn't had this dinner... but she might not have agreed to let him stay the night and spending time with his dad was important.

Had Tyra figured out that keeping a lid on their new relationship wasn't a long-term solution? Next week she'd get her truck back, eliminating her need to bum a ride from anyone, including him. Andy had only agreed to the early-morning lessons because it was crunch time and he was eager to make a good impression at Angie's birthday bash at the ranch. After that he might not care about keeping the lessons under the radar.

What a kick it would be to watch Andy busting some new moves for the family gathered at Rowdy Roost. Not possible. He'd be at the Buffalo with Tyra making sure the Valentine's gala was a huge success.

When he arrived at Kendall's place, his dad's rented Corvette looked even more incongruous parked in front of her modest little cottage. Cheyenne had made one significant change since moving in. Smoke drifted from the rock fireplace he'd built as a Christmas gift for his lady.

Of course Cheyenne hadn't gotten away with doing it alone. Their little sis Angie had insisted on lending a hand in the design and construction. Kendall, never one to stand on the sidelines, had helped haul rocks and mix cement. Cheyenne could take credit for buying all the materials, though, and Kendall was over the moon now that she finally had a fireplace.

Clint had asked what he could bring and she'd requested an apple pie from the Buffalo. Carrying the pie and a pint of vanilla ice cream he'd snagged at the Wagon Train Market right before they'd closed, he climbed the porch steps.

Cheyenne barreled out before he could cross the porch and rap on the front door. "What's the deal with Tyra?"

"It's good to see you, too, bro."

"Yeah, you, too. Come on in." He turned back and held the door. "Come on in. We're dying of curiosity here. We're getting all these conflicting reports and Dallas said she had dinner with him Thursday night, but—"

"You talked to Dallas?"

"He started his shift yesterday."

"Oh, right. I knew that. Just forgot. Anyway, what did he say?"

"That Tyra was friendly enough but she acted like a woman who had another guy on her mind. And we've pooled our info and concluded that other guy is you."

"It has to be you, Clint." Kendall came out of the kitchen. "Thanks for bringing the pie. And ice cream!" She took both. "I didn't mention ice cream because I thought you'd have to mess with dishing it into a smaller container if you brought ice cream from the Buffalo's stash."

"It was easier to grab this at the market. Hey, Dad."

"Good to see you son." His dad gave him a hug. "You didn't mention that you and Tyra had a moment on the dance floor Thursday afternoon. Wondered why you stayed behind the bar all evening."

"A moment on the dance floor?" Clint tried not to panic. "Did Rance tell you that? Because you know he exaggerates everything."

"Believe it or not," Cheyenne said, "Rance didn't mention it at all. That part of the story came courtesy of the Wenches."

Clint stifled a groan. "Were they at the Buffalo last night? I didn't see—"

"No, they weren't there," his dad said. "They all had other commitments last night. But they wanted to see me while I'm here so your mom invited them to lunch today."

"The food's ready." Cheyenne beckoned them to the kitchen. "Come fill your plates and take them into the dining room. We can talk this out once we get settled."

"You guys can get a beer from the fridge," Kendall said. "I'm having tea."

Moments later they were gathered around the cozy oval table that Kendall's grandfather had made more than fifty years ago. Clint had learned about that the first time he'd come over for dinner soon after Cheyenne moved here. The table sat four comfortably. Any more pushed the limits.

Three of them could see the fireplace from the table. Kendall had wanted it that way. When he took the seat that put his back to the fire, Cheyenne and Kendall objected. They insisted he take one of the other chairs.

Cheyenne put his back to the fireplace. "I don't have to see it. I look at it all the time."

"He does," Kendall said. "We practically live in front of that fire. When we have a blizzard, we bring our mattress out here."

"We used to do that when we were kids." Clint glanced across the table at his twin. "Wall-to-wall mattresses."

Cheyenne nodded. "And Mom refereeing when we squabbled about mattress placement." He shifted into falsetto. "*If you boys don't quit fighting, you're all going back to your rooms.*"

"That was after my time," their dad said. "Sounds like fun, though."

"It was always fun over at Rowdy Ranch." Kendall passed around a basket of hot rolls. "Be sure and have one. Cheyenne's getting really good at yeast rolls."

"Yes, I am, if I do say so myself, but let's get back to the topic at hand. I believe the story begins with your text to me asking whether Dallas was seeing anyone and whether he'd be at the gathering on Wednesday night. I take it that was all a plan to set him up with Tyra?"

"Yes. But it didn't work out."

"So Dallas said. Then she texted him that her truck broke down and you happened along and took her home. He was a little put out that she didn't call him when it happened, since she wasn't that far from his house."

"I got there right after her truck died." He held steady, determined not to give himself away. Cheyenne knew him too well, though, damn it. Better than Kendall, but even she was studying him with way too much interest.

His dad didn't seem to notice. He took a sip of his beer. "Let's not forget the high-octane dance performance on Thursday afternoon when you auditioned the new band."

Clint decided not to respond.

His father continued. "The Wenches said sparks were flying between you two. I don't doubt it. Nothing like adding sexual chemistry to partners who know how to dance."

Or maybe he would say something so they could cut to the chase. "Okay, I'm crazy about her. But as I told you yesterday morning, it's problematic. She loves the Buffalo, which is why she came home to take it over when her dad was ready to sell. A romance with me could turn sour. Then what? She's staying, regardless. If it becomes the least bit contentious between us, one of us has to give up the Buffalo. One guess who that will be. Everybody loses." Stated that way, he must be a lunatic. He should never have taken her home that first night.

"I would love to see you two together, son. I know you pretty well and I got a good sense of what she's about last night. You seem to fit. In your shoes I'd probably go for it and damn the torpedoes."

"So you said last night."

"I was tired and a little drunk. You and Tyra aren't wrong about the pitfalls. I've been on way too many sets where folks couple up and then it goes bad, throwing the whole cast into chaos. It can run up production costs, sabotage morale, even tank the entire project."

Kendall sighed. "Personally, I feel sad for Tyra."

That stumped him. "Why?"

"I always thought of her as having it all. I was a little intimidated by her. Then we got to talking last Wednesday night and I realized she's lonely."

He blinked. Lonely? Could that be true?

"I can tell from your face that you don't believe me, Clint, but think about it. She loves the town, the setting, being back among wild critters, although she admitted she hasn't had time to get out into nature that much."

"It's been an intense time while she got acclimated."

"I can only imagine. On top of that, her best friend from high school moved years ago and any others from those days are busy with kids and families. Tyra's an outlier."

Kendall had nailed that part. "She'd likely agree with you."

"She's also taken on a beloved institution that in many ways is the heart of this town and she's following in the footsteps of her father, no less. He left the business in great shape. She's petrified that she'll let him down, let Wagon Train down. She's in a vulnerable spot."

And wasn't he a prince for adding more complications and pressure? She hadn't asked him to kiss her that Tuesday morning. He'd offered. What a noble guy. She was the one who'd suggested going back to his house on Thursday night, but that didn't excuse him. He'd been all too eager to fall in with the plan. As for this morning, that was all his doing.

"I have an idea," Kendall said. "I feel like Tyra and I connected Wednesday night. She invited me to come to lunch sometime at the Buffalo. I should go. I understand the pressure of following in your dad's footsteps. I had to do that with this place after my dad died."

"You did a super job, too," Cheyenne said.

"I did okay, but it wasn't easy. I also had Angie. Tyra has you, Clint, but no offense, you're a guy."

"No offense taken."

"Will she be there tomorrow?"

"Yes."

"Is she home now?"

"She is."

"Then if you'll excuse me for a minute, I'll call her and see if tomorrow would work." She left the table and ducked into the kitchen.

Cheyenne gazed at him. "I could be wrong, but I think you're in deep."

"For what it's worth," his dad said, "he told me yesterday morning that he still had a crush but it was manageable."

Cheyenne's attention flicked to their dad and then back to him. "Is it?"

"It has to be."

"That's not really an answer. You—"

"She's available." Kendall came back in and took her seat. "We're set for noon. She asked if we were talking about her and I said we were and I'd tell her all about it tomorrow."

Clint gulped. "You will?"

"Why not? If I'd had more information earlier, I would have asked you to bring her, but maybe this is better. We'll have some girl talk at the Buffalo while you guys go on your ride."

"What ride?"

Cheyenne turned to him. "Dad and I are taking the horses out sometime in the middle of the day, when it's the warmest. If you can go, it would be... well, like old times. I planned to put Dad on Mayhem and you can have either Mischief or Black Jack. Your choice."

"I might be able to work that out. What time?"

"I was thinking around one."

"Let's do it."

"I love it when a plan comes together," Kendall said. "Dig in, everybody. We have pie warming in the oven and ice cream for dessert."

Clint ate because he refused to leave food on his plate after his brother and sister-in-law had worked hard to prepare a nice meal. He even forced down a piece of warm apple pie topped with a scoop of ice cream.

But his appetite was shot. He'd become involved with Tyra to fulfill a fantasy. How selfish was that? When he'd had doubts, he'd shoved them aside. *Live for the moment.* Yeah, right. How about this moment? Fun, huh?

He'd convinced himself that even if there were repercussions, he'd make sure they didn't cause a problem. He was playing with fire, and worse than that, he wasn't the only one who could get burned. Time to wise up.

He used a trip to the bathroom as an excuse to text Rance at the Buffalo. *Call me in 5 minutes. Say you have a problem and you need me there.*

Are you really coming in?

No. I'll explain later.

Good old Rance loved intrigue more than he loved chocolate layer cake. He texted a thumbs up emoji.

Clint rejoined the group in clearing the table and loading the dishwasher. The job went quickly. Any minute his dad would head for the coat rack. As he moved to do that, Clint's phone rang.

He pulled it out of his pocket and put it to his ear. "Hey, Rance." He bit his cheek to keep from laughing as Rance told him in a terrified whisper that the band members had turned into aliens, abducted the customers and carried them off to their home planet. "No worries. I'll be right there."

His dad glanced at him. "Problems?"

"Nothing too bad, but Rance said he'd feel better if I came in to help him deal with it. Probably just a fuse."

"I'd go in with you and keep you company, but I'm still catching up on sleep. I want to be bright-eyed and bushy-tailed for that ride tomorrow."

"That's fine, Dad. I'll see you in the morning." Yikes. He hadn't considered his dad might want to come with him. He thanked Kendall and Cheyenne for a great dinner and beat it out the door before his dad changed his mind.

<u>23</u>

Kendall's surprise phone call threw Tyra for a loop. She'd had the phone in her hand, her finger raised to tap on her dad's number. When it rang and Kendall's name popped up on the screen, she'd stared at it in confusion for a couple of seconds before she'd finally answered.

They'd exchanged numbers on Wednesday night and she'd invited Kendall to come in sometime so they could chat over lunch. But this wasn't just a casual lunch. Kendall had a purpose, to report on the discussion currently taking place around her dining table. Tyra hadn't known what to say to that.

Did she even want to know? Guaranteed they weren't talking about what kind of job she was doing as the new owner of the saloon. This had to be about whether she and Clint were romantically involved. She trusted him to finesse any questions that came his way, but that might not work with his family. They knew him too well, especially Cheyenne.

His twin would have questions about the Dallas situation. He'd been involved from the get-go, providing info on his friend and work buddy.

She'd discovered after the fact that Cheyenne and Dallas had worked the same shift on Friday.

She sighed. Her intimate encounters with Clint had remained undetected for less than forty-eight hours. How much time did they have left on the secrecy clock? Curious folks were asking questions. Multiple connections linked the townspeople in an intricate communication grid. Their cloak of invisibility would evaporate — maybe tomorrow, maybe next week, but soon.

They could wait in suspense for the inevitable moment when their liaison hit the grapevine. Or they could announce it themselves and take control of the narrative. She preferred the second option, but was she ready for that? Was he?

There was a third alternative, one that sent a stabbing pain to her chest. She could call a halt now. Tonight. Before anybody knew anything for sure. That would reduce the chance of exposure to nearly zero. Her close neighbors might suspect something, but if this morning's episode never happened again, they'd probably forget about it.

If she could bring herself to act now, she could tell Kendall tomorrow at lunch that she and Clint had decided a platonic friendship was best for all concerned. She could give her new friend permission to inform the family since there seemed to be some speculation going on.

But calling a halt tonight meant doing it by text. With Clint's dad staying with him, a phone call was too risky. Ending things with a text made her blood run cold. Unthinkable. They needed to mutually agree to it. That meant waiting until tomorrow morning, when he'd come over expecting they'd….

The ache in her chest got worse. She created a circular path in her living room and forced herself to deepen her breathing. The pacing didn't help much but it was better than standing there picturing Clint getting that text. Or appearing on her doorstep in the morning, eager to make love.

She glanced at the phone in her hand. She held it in a death grip so intense that her knuckles had turned white. Okay, she didn't need to make the decision right now. He was likely still at Kendall and Cheyenne's house finishing dinner.

She'd call her dad. With luck he was home and not too busy to talk. His voice always calmed her.

When he answered, the buzz of conversation and the clink of glasses signaled a party going on in the background. "Did I call at a bad time? Do you have company?"

"We do, honey, but your timing is perfect. I just lost my shirt in our weekly poker game. Talking to you is better than sitting at the poker table twiddling my thumbs."

"I forgot about your Saturday night poker game. Sorry."

"Hey, I don't expect you to keep track of our schedule. I'm barely able to do it. We have something going on all the time."

"That's wonderful. You sound happy, Dad." This was just the mood booster she needed.

"That's because I am happy. I never would have thought a retirement community in the desert would suit me, but it does. I even started playing golf this past week."

"*No.*"

"I'm lousy, but three friends talked me into it and they're willing to put up with my clumsy attempts. I'm taking lessons, so I should get better. But enough about me, how are things up there in snow country?"

"Snowy and cold."

"I thought as much. How're things at the Buffalo?"

"You mean the place that has a wooden mascot that talks? The one whose original voice was created by Nick Reynolds, who's passed the tradition on to his son? That Buffalo?" Clint's latest recording session had been a watershed moment. What a dope she'd been, thinking that if they talked about their attraction that would lessen its impact.

Her dad laughed. "So Nick actually made it there. He wasn't sure he could swing it. Is he still around?"

"Until Monday. Tonight he's over at Kendall and Cheyenne's having dinner. Clint's there, too." Likely picking his way through a minefield of questions.

"Was Clint bowled over when he found out? I'll bet he was."

"I'm sure he was, but I wasn't there. Nick told him when he arrived at Clint's cabin Friday morning. Then they came into town to tell me. Nick has rented — get this — a yellow Corvette. He's driving it all over the place."

"My God, the man hasn't changed a bit."

"Cecily thinks he looks even younger, probably as a result of recent plastic surgery."

"No doubt. Last time I saw him he was doing the Paul Newman trick of dunking his face in ice water every morning."

"It's weird to think you've known him all this time. You could have told me. I would have kept the secret."

"Your mother and I debated that a lot. But Nick was paranoid about SAG finding out so we deferred to his wishes. Those recordings have been great for business. I've tried to pay him since then, but he won't take it. Anyway, were you surprised to find out?"

"I was at first, but then it made sense because Clint sounds just like him." Only better. Clint's voice had a slightly rougher edge, which she found irresistible, especially when they were in—

"Tyra? Are you there?"

"Sorry, Dad. I got distracted. What did you say?"

"I just asked about the Valentine's Day shindig. Last time we talked you'd ordered a bunch of decorations."

"They look awesome, too. I'll send you pictures. And besides the decorations, Rance came up with a great idea to make the night even more special."

"Yeah? Let's hear it."

She described the door prize concept and unsurprisingly, her dad loved it. "I'm letting Rance emcee the drawing, but Clint and I will be on hand to monitor him and make sure he doesn't turn it into a game show." She and Clint would be working buddies. On Valentine's Day. Blech.

"Judging from what you've said, Rance has matured in the past couple of years."

"He has, although he's still Rance. Can't resist going for the laugh."

"Clint's the right person to ride herd on him. He had some Rance tendencies when he was younger."

"I can believe that."

"But he's grown into a helluva good guy. I'm sure you'll agree with me now that you know him so much better."

"I do agree." She barely got the words out. Then she quickly swallowed a burst of hysterical laughter.

"The two of you make a terrific team. I rest easy down here, knowing the Buffalo's in good hands. I didn't want to own it anymore, but I didn't want it to go down the tubes. The town wouldn't be the same without that place."

"I promise to keep it going strong, Dad." *Whatever it takes.*

"I know you will, sweetheart. I never had any doubt. You'll handle it the way you've handled everything you ever took on. I'm a very proud papa. You'd blush if you heard how I brag about you to the folks down here."

"Then it's a good thing they've never met me. They'd probably expect Wonder Woman in a spandex suit."

"You used to have one of those."

"Yeah, when I was eight."

"I think of you as Wonder Woman, only with red—hey, excuse me for a sec. Somebody's trying to get my attention."

"Sure thing."

After some noisy comments and laughter in the background, he came back. "Evidently I'm expected to mix up a batch of my famous margaritas."

"I remember those. You started me on the virgin ones."

"I taught Clint how to make 'em. You should get him to mix you up a batch."

"I just might do that." No, and hell, no. She was in enough trouble already. Clint and a pitcher of margaritas would be a lethal combination.

"Tell him hello for me. Gotta sign off. Love you, honey."

"Love you, too, Dad." She disconnected. Well, there it was. Her father had entrusted the Buffalo to her, knowing she'd bring her A game and she'd be assisted by the best manager a girl could ask for.

Yes, he was easy on the eyes and he could dampen her panties with a look. But her admiration for Clint went way beyond his sex appeal. The man had substance. He'd worked as hard or sometimes harder than she had these past two years without a single complaint. He looked for ways to lighten the mood and make her laugh whenever the going got tough. He didn't expect huge doses of praise for his efforts. He was exactly what her dad had said — a helluva good guy.

He cared more about the welfare of the Buffalo than the paycheck he received from it. She was the official owner, but he was its heart and soul. The town wouldn't be the same without the Buffalo, but the Buffalo wouldn't be the same without Clint.

Knowing all that should make her decision easy. She had the perfect setup to make the Buffalo even more successful than it already was. Only a fool would take a chance on messing things up. She might have already done it, but they'd kept this situation somewhat contained. If she—

The knock at the door made her jump and turn in that direction.

"Tyra, it's me."

"Clint?" She rushed to open the door. "What are you doing here? And where's your truck?"

"I parked around the corner. Can I come in?"

"Sure." She opened the door and stepped back, heart pounding. Why did he have to look so...lovable? "But I don't under—"

"No one knows I'm here."

"How can that be? You were just with your dad, Kendall and Cheyenne." She closed the door and turned, disoriented by his sudden appearance.

He unzipped his jacket but didn't take it off. "As the meal was winding down, I secretly texted Rance and told him to call me with a fake emergency at the Buffalo. When I got his call, I made my excuses and drove straight here. I texted Rance that I'm not coming to the Buffalo and I'll fill him in later."

"Fill him in on what?" He wasn't here to make love. Keeping his jacket on told her that. He was out of breath, though, and he'd shoved his hands in his pockets, not in a casual way, either.

A muscle twitched in his jaw. "Some version of what I'm about to say. He doesn't need details. No one does. But they shouldn't be surprised that I needed to talk this out with you in person."

She began to shake. "You still haven't told me—"

"It won't be easy for either of us, but we have to stop..." He swallowed. "We're taking a big personal risk, but that's not all. We're risking the fate of the Buffalo. We don't have that right. Or I should say, *I* don't have that right."

Her throat hurt but she managed to get the words out. "Neither do I."

"You agree with me?" His gaze was bleak.

She nodded, grief curdling in her stomach. "I should never have suggested going back to your house."

"I should never have gone along with it. The chance to live out my fantasy was so tempting. That's not an excuse. I selfishly gave in to it. I should have been stronger."

"Please don't beat yourself up. I shouldn't have put you in that position."

His gaze flickered, a faint glow in his eyes for the first time since he'd walked in. "For the record, I enjoyed every single position you put me in."

She stared at him. "Did you just make a joke?"

"Somebody had to." His expression softened. "If we're gonna get through this, and we are, we'll need some jokes along the way."

The tightness in her chest gave way a little. "Then here's one for you. When I walked over to the *Sentinel* office today, I made a detour and stopped by the drugstore to make a purchase."

His breath caught. "Is that so?"

"And now that box won't be opened."

His blue eyes darkened to navy. "That's a shame after you went to all that trouble."

Heat shot through her veins. "But we just decided—"

"Yes, ma'am. And that decision will take effect when I walk out your front door. In the meantime, the emergency at the Buffalo might take longer than I anticipated." He held her gaze. "Or I can leave now. Your choice."

24

Tyra stood very still. Only the turmoil in her eyes reflected the battle raging inside. Guilt punched Clint in the gut. Was this suggestion another selfish move on his part? "Never mind. Bad idea." He headed for the door.

"Don't go."

He turned around. "If you're struggling with the choice, the answer should be no. I'll—"

"I really want to. But won't that make it harder?"

Serious moment, but... what the hell. "Yes, ma'am, I reckon it will." He gazed at her. "In fact, I sincerely hope so."

She choked out a laugh. "You're such a doofus."

"So I've been told." He flashed her a grin as he left his jacket and hat on the coat tree. "But you must admit I'll require that condition for those little raincoats you bought." Crossing the room, he held out his hand.

She slipped her fingers through his. "I didn't say what was in the box." Leading him toward the staircase, she threw a saucy glance over her shoulder. "Maybe I bought you Valentine candy."

"Whatever's in that box, I'll work with it." He squeezed her hand. "Pick up the pace, lady. I can't wait to undress you. Never got to do that." Looked like he'd have one chance at that experience. He'd make the most of it.

When she ran up the stairs, he stayed with her, even though his fly pinched and his heart ached so bad it took his breath away. Soon she'd be in his arms and his jeans would cease to be a problem. The warmth of her body pressed against his would ease the ache in his heart. He'd live in the moment.

She pulled him through the doorway of her dark bedroom and let go of his hand. "You turn on the lamps, I'll get the shades."

"Yes, ma'am. I want plenty of light."

"I picked up on that." She lowered the first shade as he switched on the lamp closest to the door.

Rounding the bed, he followed her, clicking the second lamp switch at the same time she pulled down the second shade. He chuckled. "Damn, we're efficient."

"And synchronized." She turned around, only inches away, and tipped up her face to his. "I want to undress you, too, you know. Maybe we should flip a coin to see who goes—"

"Better let me. We know what happens when you get your hands on me."

"Sounds like you want to take it slow for a change."

"It's a goal. Might not happen, but let's try."

"Okay." She rested her hands on his shoulders.

His nostrils flared. "You smell delicious." Taking hold of her wrist, he unfastened the button on the cuff of her silky black shirt.

"It's the vegetable soup. I finished the last of it for supper."

"It's not the soup." He pressed his lips to the rapid pulse beating just under the surface. "It's you." His groin tensed. *Slow down.* He breathed deep as he pushed back her sleeve and kissed his way up to the tender spot inside her elbow.

She trembled. "I'm not wearing perfume."

"You don't need to." Lowering her arm, he reached for her other wrist and slipped the button free. "You always smell great." He drew her sleeve back gently, allowing the soft material to stroke her skin. Her breathing quickened as he ran his tongue from her wrist to her elbow. "I remember that from when we waited tables together."

"You were never close enough."

"Oh, yeah, I was. I'd deliberately bump into you." He reached for the top button of her shirt.

"I thought you were clumsy."

"Infatuated." He moved with deliberate care down the row of buttons, brushing his knuckles over her satin skin, savoring the warmth, the slight hitch in her breath every time he made contact. "I was obsessed with your smile, the way your ponytail swung as you rushed back and forth between the dining room and the kitchen, the tunes you hummed under your breath when you bussed a table."

"You remember me humming?"

"I was paying attention." He finished unbuttoning her shirt and slipped it off, tossing it toward a nearby chair.

"I kinda knew."

"I wasn't subtle. I followed your every move."

"And you were cute as hell. But...too young."

"Not too young to dream." He slid his hands behind her back. "Especially when you'd whisk by and gave me a wink. I lived for those winks."

"I shouldn't have done that."

"I loved it." He dragged in a breath. "But I love this more." He unhooked her bra and pulled it slowly away, keeping his gaze locked with hers as he flung the bra toward the chair.

"Me, too." Anticipation shimmered in the emerald depths of her eyes.

"Step over here, pretty lady." Heart hammering, he edged backward, drawing her with him. When he made contact with the mattress, he sat down, spread his knees and pulled her in close. Saliva pooled in his mouth as he gazed at the bounty before him. "If you don't mind, I'd like to hang out here a while."

Her rapid breathing made her breasts quiver. "I don't mind." She gasped when he cradled her breasts in his hands and placed a kiss on each nipple. "But we know what happens when you get your hands on me."

"That's my line."

"Works both ways."

"But you have orgasms to spare." And he settled in. Loving her like this delivered amazing pleasure to his mouth and intense pain for his cock. The tradeoff was worth it, especially when she clutched the back of his head and arched her back, letting him know he was giving as well as getting.

Gradually her whimpers became more urgent. Her fingertips pressing against his scalp left him free to release his hold, undo her jeans and give her what she needed. She was almost there. He barely had to touch her and she erupted with a gasp and a triumphant cry of release.

Music to his ears. He steadied her when the aftershocks left her wobbly. Rising carefully to his feet, he drew her close, reversed their positions and eased her down to the bed.

She gazed up at him, her lush mouth curved in a smile. "That was lovely. But now I'm all limp and trembly. You might have to take your own clothes off."

"Works for me, but I'm not quite finished with yours." He drank in the sight of her lying there all flushed and satisfied. Beautiful. Pain sliced through his chest. He swallowed. It was part of the price and he was willing to pay it.

She started to sit up. "I can—"

"Nope. My job." Her legs still dangled over the edge of the bed. He sent an apology to his privates and crouched down to pull off her boots and socks. "Such pretty feet." So little time. So much to memorize. He kissed each toe.

She giggled. "That tickles."

"Are you ticklish?" He didn't know. What other things had he missed and now would never learn?

"Only my feet."

He couldn't resist brushing his fingers lightly over her toes.

She jerked her feet away. "No fair. Now you have to tell me if you're ticklish so I can get revenge."

"Under my ribs. And now I'll be on my guard." But they didn't have time for a tickling contest.

"I'm sneaky. You'll never see it coming."

"Good luck with that." Grasping her jeans and the waistband of her panties, he divested her of both. "I play a mean tickle defense."

"I'll bet I could take you."

"Many have tried. Few have succeeded." But she would. When it came to Tyra, he had no defenses. Leaving her jeans and panties on the nearby chair, he used it for balance as he toed off his boots. Then he turned toward the bed while he popped the snaps on his shirt. The view in that direction was way better.

She rose to her elbows. "Stop."

"Change your mind about doing this?"

"No. But I want to watch." Swinging her feet up on the bed, she tugged the covers out from under her and tossed them back. Then she stretched out on her side, grabbed a pillow and used it to support her head.

He smiled. "Ready, now?"

"Proceed. But you can go fast if you want. Looking at your sexy self standing there, I'm finding my second wind."

"Good to know." *Keep it light. That's how we'll survive this.* He pulled his partly unbuttoned shirt over his head and let it fall to the floor. "Just out of curiosity, where's this mystery box you picked up today?"

"The one that may or may not contain Valentine candy?"

"Uh-huh. It might come in handy. Or not. Depends on what's in it." He unbuckled his belt and reached for the button on his jeans.

"Let's find out, shall we?" Her attention on his fly as he eased down the zipper, she scooted closer to the edge of the bed and fumbled for the handle on the nightstand drawer. She found it and opened the drawer.

He wasn't close enough to see what was in there but if she'd bought a heart-shaped box of Valentine candy, he was Bugs Bunny. Shoving down his jeans and briefs, he let out a sigh of relief and kicked them away.

"Oh, my, look at that." She focused on his cock. "I hope the ones I got aren't too small."

Uh-oh. He hadn't factored in that potential. If the damned things didn't fit....

"We'll hope for the best. Here you go." She lobbed the box in his direction. Sort of.

He lunged, scooping it up before it hit the floor. Then he looked at it. "Hey, you got the exact same ones I—"

"You're not the only person who pays attention."

"You checked out the box at my house?" He slit the protective shrink wrap with his thumbnail.

"Just in case."

The ache in his heart came back full force. She'd nourished the same flicker of hope he had. Otherwise she wouldn't have bothered with that detail. Taking out a foil package, he ripped it open.

"After this morning's episode I decided that I needed to be prepared." She gave him a bright smile. "And here we are. Prepared."

Nope. Not even slightly. When she'd bought the condoms, she'd believed in the impossible. Tonight she'd lost that belief. So had he. And a gaping hole had opened up in his heart, one that might never be filled.

"Get over here, cowboy," she murmured. "Don't give out on me, now."

Lifting his head, he sucked in a breath. "Never, sweet lady." Holding her gaze, he approached the bed. The glow in her emerald eyes strengthened his resolve as he climbed into bed and moved over her. "Never in a million years."

He sank into her warmth slowly, absorbing the sensation, letting it soak into his body, his heart, his soul. This was it. This moment had to last him the rest of his life.

She rubbed his back, her breathing deep and steady except for the little gasp when he gave one final push, touching the entrance to her womb. How could it be the last time? But it was. He could see it in her eyes. Surely she could see it in his.

Moving gently, he began to stroke. He kept the pace easy. When his climax shouldered its way forward, he shoved it back.

She gulped as a tremor rolled over his cock. "Whoops." She licked her lips. "I don't want to come."

"I don't either."

"Slow down some more."

He eased off. Then he clenched his jaw when her channel tightened again.

"Oh, Clint." She began to pant. "I'm trying, but I can't...hold back. I'm sorry."

"Don't be sorry." He thrust faster. "Go for it. I'll see if I can hold off." But when she came apart in his arms, his body betrayed him. With a harsh cry, he buried himself deep, silently swearing a blue streak as he surrendered to the inevitable. It was over.

And she was crying, damn it. Leaning down, he kissed her wet cheeks. "It'll be okay."

She nodded, but the tears continued to dribble from the corners of her eyes as she hugged him close.

"We'll—" He cleared the hoarseness from his throat. "We'll help each other through it."

"I know." She swallowed.

"One day at a time."

"R-Right." She sniffed and tightened her grip.

He didn't want to leave this bed any more than she wanted him to, but the moment had to happen. Raising his head, he looked into her eyes. They still glistening with tears. "You need to turn me loose."

She sniffed again. "Don't want to."

"I'll bring you a box of tissues."

She managed a tiny smile. "Tired of listening to me sniff?"

"No, but sniffing's not doing the job."

"Snot's running out of my nose?"

"Just a little bit."

"Why didn't you tell me?"

"I just did."

"Thanks a lot. Now when you think of this moment, you'll be thinking of snot."

"You have lovely snot."

Her giggle was watery, but at least he'd made her laugh. She released her hold and he anchored the condom firmly as he eased away from her. Better make sure they didn't accidentally—

The minute the concept popped into his head, he shoved it away. There was a topic that could drive him completely around the bend. He washed up, grabbed the box of tissues on the bathroom counter and walked back into the bedroom.

She'd left the bed and started getting dressed. She'd made it as far as her bra and panties.

"You don't have to get dressed." He handed her the box.

"Yes, I do. And thanks." She pulled out a tissue and set the box on the chair while she blew her nose.

"Why not stay here? I can lock you in when I leave."

Balling up the tissue, she tossed it in a wastebasket next to the chair. Then she met his gaze. "I'm walking you to the door."

"But—"

"And kissing you goodbye."

"You can do that now."

"No, I can't." She perched on the end of the chair while she pulled on her socks. "If I kiss you while we're in here, we'll be back in that bed in no time. If we're both dressed and standing by the door, we'll manage to behave."

"All right." He hadn't figured on a last kiss. Could make it tougher to walk out that door. But since he'd been the genius who'd suggested one last shot at making love, he wasn't about to deny her one last kiss.

25

After Tyra finished dressing, she grabbed the brush from her dresser and ran it through her hair while Clint silently put on his clothes. The swish of the brush and the pop of snaps locking into place were the only sounds in the room.

He might not be happy with the idea of one last kiss, but she refused to let him leave her house with a vivid image of her teary eyes and runny nose. She'd gathered her forces since then. She'd be able to kiss him once more without crying.

He tucked in his shirt, fastened the metal button at the waist of his jeans, zipped up and buckled his belt. Familiar motions she'd never see again. Uh-oh. She had a lump in her throat. Not good. But she wasn't giving up that last kiss, damn it. She swallowed hard.

His husky voice broke the silence. "Let's go."

Better not look at him until they reached her front door. "Okay." She walked out of the room and he followed.

"I just realized you'll need a ride in the morning. I can—"

"Thanks, but I won't need one." Her stomach churned. How like him to offer, despite everything. "I don't actually have to come in until I meet Kendall for lunch. I'll ask her to pick me up."

"That works." His boots on the steps created a steady tempo instead of the rapid beat when he'd raced upstairs with her. "I should give you back your key."

"Not necessarily. If you have a key, you can record when I'm not here."

"Oh." A pause. "We're caught up for now. Maybe by the time we need another recording, we'll be more—"

"There's St. Patrick's Day. We need an updated version in about three weeks."

"Right. I forgot about that one." He sighed. "I'll keep the key."

When she reached the bottom of the stairs, she zeroed in on his jacket and hat hanging on the coat tree. Damn, her eyes were watering again. She swiped at them with both hands as she crossed to the door.

"Tyra." The kind way he said it plucked at her heartstrings.

"What?"

"Don't do this to yourself. Go into the kitchen and close the door. You don't have to—"

"Yes, I do." Blinking away the blasted tears, she spun around to face him. "I have something to say and after tonight, I won't have the chance."

The sadness in his eyes turned them almost gray. "Come to think of it, I have something to say, too." He cleared his throat. "You first."

She nodded. Breathed deep. "I take full responsibility for—"

"Hang on. You can't—"

"I sure can. When my truck broke down, you kept insisting on taking me home. If I'd let you do that, we wouldn't be standing here feeling like crap."

"So you regret what happened?" Pain laced his words. "Because I—"

"No. I'm just saying—"

"That you take responsibility? Isn't that regret?"

"No! But if it weren't for me—"

"If it weren't for you, we wouldn't have made love." He moved closer, got right in her face. "And that's what *I* want to say. This part is awful, but—""

"I *know*, and I'm so sorry that—"

"Listen to me, Tyra." His voice shook. "You want to take responsibility? Then take responsibility for giving me more pleasure than I ever thought possible. Making love with you has been the highlight of my life."

She gulped. "Really?"

"Really. I'm a lucky guy." He pulled her close. "Yeah, we'll have some awkward moments as we stumble through this, but we'll handle it." He kissed her with infinite tenderness, holding her gently but firmly in his arms.

She kissed him back, hugging him closer than she should, while tears dripped down her cheeks.

He let her go slowly and reached for his jacket and hat. His steady gaze filled with a warm light as he backed toward the door. Reaching behind him, he opened it. "Be seeing you." He stepped outside and pulled the door closed with a muted click.

Gone.

26

"Basically, Clint and I came to the conclusion that the potential disruption to the Buffalo wasn't worth it." Tyra's bowl of chili sat in front of her, untouched, but getting this discussion with Kendall out of the way took priority. After saying her piece, she'd eat it, not that she had any appetite.

Clint and Rance were behind the bar, yukking it up. If she had a good joke to go along with her explanation to Kendall, she'd be trotting it out right now. Maybe Kendall would bring up the comic side of this situation so they could sit over here laughing their heads off, too.

But Kendall looked bewildered instead of amused. She cocked her head to one side. "Huh. So you decided this together?"

"Yes. Yes, we did."

"When? Because at our place last night, things still seemed like they were up in the air. That's what I was going to report to you today. Clint admitted he was crazy about you."

She swallowed. "I like him a lot, too. But we both knew the risk to the business. He came by last night to discuss it." The supposed emergency at the

Buffalo could do double duty. If Clint was smart, and he definitely was, he'd told Rance the same thing. Maybe they were cracking up over the fake emergency call, although it couldn't be *that* funny.

"Oh, you mean after he handled whatever went wrong here?"

"Uh-huh." A tiny lie.

"That's certainly mature of you guys."

"In the end, it was an easy decision." A bigger lie. "We both love the Buffalo. It's been part of my life since I was little. Same with Clint. His dad used to bring him and Cheyenne here as a special treat whenever he came to town."

"Nick mentioned that to me. He loves the Buffalo, too. Fascinating guy, fun to be with, but I can see why Desiree refused to marry him. She'd have added one more kid to her brood."

Tyra smiled. Now they were on safer ground. "Did he tell you she turned him down flat?"

"Oh, yes. He's a great storyteller. And he admits it wouldn't have worked. He's not cut out for marriage, which he proved by having three failed ones. Thank goodness Cheyenne doesn't take after him. Clint's a little more like his dad in the way he loves to kid around."

"Yeah, he does." Back on rocky ground. It was one of the things she cherished about him.

"But when Clint gets attached to something, he stays attached. Like his family. Like this town. Like the Buffalo."

Her chest tightened, making it hard to breathe. "Yep." There had to be an elegant way to switch topics, but damned if she could come up with one.

Kendall's gaze filled with sympathy. "You said the decision was easy, but I can tell it wasn't."

"No." She bunched her napkin in her lap and took a quick breath. "But..." She grabbed a little more air. "It's the right one."

"I get it. After my dad died, it was like this huge weight landed on my shoulders. He'd worked so hard to keep our little ranch going and now it was my job. I couldn't let him down."

"I know how that feels." The tightness in her chest eased.

"I'm sure you do."

"I didn't have to take this on, but I thought I did."

"Of course you had to. You didn't want it going to some out-of-town stranger who could change the whole character of the place."

"Turns out it wouldn't have. If I hadn't come back to take over, Clint was prepared to borrow enough to make a sizable down payment."

Kendall's jaw dropped. "I didn't know that. Did he tell Frank?"

"He didn't get the chance. I was the first person my dad contacted when he made the decision to sell. I was the only one who knew, besides my stepmother, of course. I asked him to hold off telling anybody else for twenty-four hours. The next day I called back and announced I was coming home."

"I'll bet he was happy."

"Overjoyed. Tearful. He'd always dreamed of giving me the Buffalo, but never said anything because I seemed so determined to take a different path."

"But didn't he buy a house down in Arizona? If he didn't get cash from the sale of the Buffalo or the sale of his house, for that matter, how did he—"

"My dad's loaded. This place has been a gold mine and he's squirreled away the profits for years. He was going to give me the money from the house and the Buffalo. He said it was my rightful inheritance. He told me that when he called to say he was selling."

"Wow. You would have made out, girlfriend."

"And lost something precious to me."

"Although Clint would have—"

"I didn't know that. Besides, I'd been thinking of moving back, anyway. I just hadn't figured out how to make a living. Wagon Train has one lawyer and he's semi-retired."

"Correction, we now have two lawyers. You're doing that pro bono thing for the wildlife folks."

"Will be doing. I haven't taken the bar exam yet."

Kendall waved a hand. "Details. You'll take it, pass it and have fun exercising your lawyer brain. I mean, you enjoyed that, right?"

"Sure."

"But do you enjoy being in charge of the Buffalo's welfare? Or is the responsibility dragging you down?"

Was it? She glanced around at the heart garlands she and Clint had hung on Tuesday, the cupids Rance had brought over to decorate the antique bar, the bandstand where House Wine would be playing again tonight.

Then she looked at Kendall, who hadn't touched her chili, either. Their meals would be lukewarm by now. "I dearly love this place. I love the scent of the wood mixed with the aroma of beer, the yummy smells from the kitchen, the scarred dance floor, the smoothness of the bar, my dad's old desk, the buzz of conversation, the music. Just being here makes me happy."

"And *I'm* happy to hear you say that. I was worried that you regretted your decision, especially since Clint would have taken care of the Buffalo if you hadn't."

"But it would have been his and not mine. I'm glad I own it. Now that I'm here, I can't imagine a different scenario. I—" Her heart rate sped up. Clint was on his way over to their table.

He wore his typical jaunty smile but he didn't look at her. "How's lunch going?"

Kendall jumped in with enthusiasm. "Great!"

"Don't see how that's possible." He surveyed the bowls of chili. "Your coffee is just sitting there getting cold and neither of you have eaten a thing, not even a hot roll. Those are definitely stone cold by now."

"We've been talking." Kendall picked up a roll. "And these aren't stone cold."

"But they sure as hell aren't hot."

"They're just fine." She bit into it. "Mm."

"This is ridiculous. I'll get Cecily to bring you hot coffee and take your chili back to warm it up."

Tyra gave him a quick glance. "No need. We're fine."

"If you say so." He rolled his eyes. "Anyway, I forgot to mention that I'm heading out to the ranch for about three hours or so. Should be back by four at the latest."

"Okay."

Kendall finished off her roll. "Cheyenne's taking Nick and Clint out riding this afternoon."

"Should be fun." Even though she avoided meeting his gaze, she still had goosebumps just because he was only inches away. And breathing.

"It's been years since we took a ride together. I'm looking forward to it."

His voice sent shivers up her spine. "See you at four, then."

"If you need someone to take you home..."

"Thanks, but I'm good."

"Then I'll catch you later. Hey, Kendall, please get Cecily to—"

"I will, Clint." She gave him a smile. "Have fun."

"Yes, ma'am." He touched the brim of his hat and walked away.

Kendall leaned across the table and lowered her voice. "Excuse me saying so, but you two are going to have to do better than that or folks will notice you're on the outs."

She closed her eyes and sighed. "I know." Gazing at Kendall, she searched for the right words. "It's just that I—"

"Love him?"

She gulped and shook her head. "No. No, I don't."

"Could've fooled me."

27

A brisk ride on a spirited horse gave Clint the lift he needed before he tackled informing his brother and dad about the current state of affairs. His brief contact with Tyra at the Buffalo hadn't been promising. She'd acted like a robot and he'd almost lost his temper.

But he'd paint a rosier picture when he described their mutual decision to his dad and Cheyenne. Unfortunately, Kendall had witnessed the frosty exchange and would likely report it to Cheyenne. Oh, well, it was a work in progress.

His dad broached the subject while they unsaddled and brushed the horses, but he asked to postpone the discussion until they were inside with a hot cup of coffee. He hadn't counted on Kendall arriving home just as they settled around the small kitchen table.

"Pour me some coffee, please," she called out from the living room. "I'll be right in."

Damn. Now he'd have to pray that his story would match with Tyra's.

The kitchen table was a tighter fit than the one in the dining room, but they managed. Kendall loaded a plate with sugar cookies from the cookie jar and handed it to Cheyenne. His twin doted on those cookies.

Clint liked them, too, and maybe a sugar high was a better idea than getting drunk, a possibility that he'd considered for tonight after work. Once everyone was settled and others had helped themselves to the cookies, he took a couple.

Kendall asked about the ride and his dad raved about it. Gratifying to hear, especially for Cheyenne who'd set it up, but Kendall didn't seem absorbed by the recitation. Instead of focusing on his dad, she kept peering at him like he was a bug under a microscope.

Finally they exhausted the topic of the ride and he decided to nudge things in the direction he needed them to go. He returned Kendall's stare. "How did it go after I left?"

"I got Cecily to warm up our chili."

"That's good."

Cheyenne blinked. "She served you cold chili?"

"It was hot to begin with. Tyra and I got to talking and forgot to eat it." She continued studying him like a science experiment. "So you went back to Tyra's house after the emergency was over?"

"Yes, ma'am." A trickle of sweat ran down his spine.

"And you two had a cozy chat and decided to put the kibosh on hanky-panky?"

"That's right." He shifted in his chair.

"You've got to be kidding." His dad put down his coffee. "Nobody has a polite discussion about something like that. Admit it. You had a fight."

"We did not." He glanced at Kendall. "Did she say we—"

"No, she said you came to a mutual decision. It sounded like an announcement following international peace talks."

Cheyenne shook his head. "I'm with Dad. You had a fight."

"No, we didn't. We're in complete agreement." He sighed. "Kendall might think we did because of the way we behaved today. We weren't as comfortable with each other as we used to be. But I promise you we didn't fight and we'll get back to normal...soon"

"Actually," Kendall said, "I don't think you had a fight."

He held his breath. If she'd somehow guessed what had gone on....

"But I do think you have a major problem."

He relaxed a little bit. "Like what?"

"When you said last night that you're crazy about her, what does that mean, exactly?"

Oh, boy. How to hedge his bets? "Along with everyone else, I think she's terrific. We all agree she's—"

"I'm not taking a poll. I'm asking you. To me, being crazy about someone is a lot more personal than thinking they're terrific. Does she turn you on?"

"With all due respect, that's none of your business." The trail of sweat down his back grew. His brother and his dad were smiling. Those two rats were getting a kick out of this.

"Which means she does." Kendall speared him with a look. "Are you in love with her?"

"Also none of your business."

"Which tells me you are. So put this in your pipe and smoke it. She's in love with you, too."

He gasped. "She *said* that?"

"Of course not. But I had a ringside seat while the two of you stumbled through that stilted conversation today. I've never seen two people more miserable. Or more in love. You may be in *complete agreement.*" She used her fingers to make air quotes. "But you guys have a big, fat mess on your hands."

28

Clint was extremely fond of his sister-in-law, but she'd just made his life a living hell. How was he supposed to coexist with Tyra now? He'd be analyzing every move she made and every conversation they had for signs that she either was or wasn't in love with him.

That would likely put her on edge, as if she wasn't, already. And if it turned out she was in love with him like Kendall said, then what? Having him around would be a constant stressor.

That was the last thing he wanted. Would he have to quit in order to remove that stress from her life? He had no good answers and plenty of lousy ones. And he really didn't want to face her right now.

Fortunately, she was on her way out the door when he got back. Cecily was taking her home. Even better, the next day was Monday, her day off. For the first time since she'd arrived two years ago, he was glad she wasn't coming in. He wouldn't have to see her again until mid-afternoon on Tuesday after Angie's birthday ride and the festivities that would follow. With luck, by then he'd have a game plan.

He scheduled a nostalgic lunch at the Buffalo with his dad and Cheyenne and requested they avoid discussing his situation with Tyra. Instead they spent the entire time reminiscing. His dad even refrained from words of advice before he climbed into the Corvette and drove back to Missoula for his flight.

Tuesday morning dawned clear and cold. The weather always seemed to cooperate for Angie's birthday. Even when it snowed, it was never enough to force a cancellation of this family tradition.

Clint vowed to put aside his own troubles and concentrate on celebrating his little sis turning twenty-five. God, that seemed young. Angie, of course, didn't consider herself young, especially now that she was the proud owner of Wagon Train Handywomen with Kendall as her trusty assistant.

As Sam dashed around looking for pets and doggie treats, the horses were brought out and saddled. Then Andy drove in, clearly eager for his first family ride.

After he parked his truck, he sought out Clint and pulled him aside. "I'm feeling good about the dancing tonight. I can't tell you how grateful I am for those three lessons."

"You're so welcome." The first one had been fun. The last two he'd had to dig deep for the necessary enthusiasm, but evidently he'd pulled it off. "Wish I could be there to watch."

"I was thinking I'd ask Jess to take a video on her phone."

"Good idea."

"Oh, hey. Kendall and Cheyenne just rode in and they've got Mayhem. Those horses look ready to party with the ribbons braided into their manes and tails. It's a nice touch."

"We like it."

"I can't wait for this ride. I'd better go over and get acquainted with my horse." He hurried off.

Clint finished saddling KoKo before joining the rest of the family digging in the ribbon box his mom brought out every year. KoKo looked a lot like his famous namesake, Rex Allen's horse. With his chocolate coat, white mane and tail, he didn't need much embellishment, so Clint only used red ribbons.

When he finished, he looked around to see if anyone needed a hand. Not far away, Dallas was struggling with the braiding routine. He'd be riding a horse Beau had borrowed from a client. Clint started over to help, but Angie beat him to it, the bouquet of ribbons on her hat bouncing as she lengthened her stride.

"Looks like you could use some assistance, Dallas."

He brightened at her approach. "Yes, ma'am. Never done anything like this."

"It's not that hard." Moving in beside him, she thumbed back her hat so she could demonstrate the braiding technique.

Clint watched with interest. Dallas had lived on the ranch for months and, although Angie had never been rude to him, she'd also never sought him out, let alone chosen to invade his space. Pretending to fix a section of KoKo's mane, he kept an eye on his little sis.

She flashed Dallas a smile. "Got it?"

"I think so."

"Give it a shot." She watched him closely. A little too closely, in Clint's opinion.

"How's that?"

"Perfect." She smiled again. "Keep going." Instead of walking away now that she'd put him on the right track, she began chatting about the ride and the pot-bellied pig race that Beau had planned again this year. Dallas acted like he was enjoying the conversation. A lot.

Clint swept a glance over the milling horses and riders until he located Cheyenne, who was helping Andy into the saddle. Beau and Jess were over there, too, along with his mom, who was holding Maverick. He led KoKo in that direction.

About the time he arrived at the fringe of the group, Andy decided he'd take a practice ride over to the corral and back. His mom turned her attention to loading Maverick into Beau's backpack, a maneuver that required some help from Jess.

While they were occupied, Clint caught Cheyenne's eye and motioned him over.

His twin lifted his eyebrows. "What?"

"Angie's making nice with Dallas."

"What do you mean *making nice?*"

"She's acting like she's interested in him. And vice versa."

"Oh, really?" He folded his arms. "Well, he's too old for her."

"I agree, but you'd better be careful who you say that to. She's not much younger than Kendall and he's only a year older than we are."

"That still makes them two years farther apart than Kendall and me. That's significant."

"What's really significant is her flirting with someone who's from here. And by *here,* I mean right down the road. She doesn't do that. She dates guys from out of town. We might see them once or twice and then they're gone."

"Maybe she's just being super nice because he's never been on one of these rides."

"Maybe. Just thought you'd want to know."

"Thanks. I'll keep my eyes and ears open. He's too old for her. If necessary, I'll say something to him." He lowered his voice. "FYI, Beau told me there's been some talk about you and Tyra."

"What kind of talk?"

"He wasn't specific. Just that folks are worried about...uh-oh." He looked over Clint's shoulder. "Hey, Andy, great job! You might want to pull back on Mayhem's reins so you don't— hang on, I'm coming."

As Cheyenne jogged off, Clint turned in time to see Andy and Mayhem ride through the open barn door. Andy had to duck to avoid banging his head.

His mom laughed. "I'll bet that old girl's just cold and tired of wandering around. We need to get this show on the road. Angie? Where's Angie? Grab Buttermilk and lead us out of here, Birthday Girl."

"On my way, Mom!" She hurried over and mounted the Buckskin named after Dale Evans' horse. "Forward, Ho!" Nudging Buttermilk into a trot, she sang the first line of the Happy Birthday tune, substituting *me* for *you.*

Everyone joined her, singing at the top of their lungs and sending clouds of vapor into the air as they took their designated places. It was determined by birth order, except for their mother, who followed directly behind Angie, and Andy, who got to be third in line since he was a parent and grandparent, too.

During last week's party, the family had voted on Dallas's place in line. He was assigned the spot between Beau and Clint, but he'd objected, saying that he should be last since he wasn't a true relative. He'd been overruled.

When he rode up to the line, Clint smiled and waved him in ahead of KoKo. Dallas touched the brim of his hat and took his place. Although he couldn't braid worth a damn, he looked at ease in the saddle and happy to be included in a family event.

He was a decent guy. He'd back off the minute Cheyenne took him aside and made that request. Problem solved.

If only all problems were that simple.

29

Tyra's nerves twanged like an out-of-tune guitar. Clint's absence for three hours Sunday and several more today reminded her how much she depended on his steady presence. Thank goodness nothing had gone seriously wrong. Yet.

Her spectacular Valentine's Day decorations had brought in a larger than usual lunch crowd, mostly older folks who'd rather celebrate early. Because they were in a party mood, most of them ordered specialty drinks. She hadn't counted on that and their relatively new bartender struggled in a situation that would have been easy for either Clint or Rance.

Cecily ended up pitching in behind the bar and Tyra dusted off her skills to help Pam, their other server, take and deliver orders. Then Vern, usually unflappable, lost patience with his new assistant when some lunch orders got mixed up in the kitchen. Two were sent back as unacceptable.

Tyra smoothed over the mistakes with discounts and gift certificates, so no one left angry, but she didn't have time to straighten out whatever issues were going on in the kitchen. Clint was great at handling personnel problems.

On one hand, she was eager for him to walk through the service door. On the other, she was afraid she'd react poorly. Kendall had a valid point. Sunday's behavior wouldn't fly with the customers.

Clint and her dad had made a good team that had created a warm and welcoming atmosphere. She and Clint had functioned the same way, maybe even better since business had picked up since she'd come on board. For one thing, she'd ramped up the decorating effort for each holiday and today proved how popular that was.

She headed toward the kitchen to place another order and pick up two. She wouldn't let this happen to her staff again. From now on she'd be prepared for a big lunch crowd on holidays, folks who tended to order fancy drinks instead of beer and wine. She and Clint might need to send their bartender for extra training, since Clint didn't really have time to train—

And there he was, striding through the back door with Rance on his heels. Her breath caught. He'd never looked more handsome. Or more out of reach. Grief sent a sharp pain arrowing through her chest.

He frowned and hurried toward her. "Are you okay?"

She nodded. "I just... it's been a hectic day." She'd unconsciously pressed the empty serving tray to her chest. Lowering it, she took a quick breath. "I didn't anticipate that lunch would be nuts. Excuse me for a minute. I need to place an order."

"You're waiting tables?"

"Yes, and Cecily's helping behind the bar. And Vern's in a mood."

Taking off his jacket and hat, Clint handed them to Rance. "Please hang these up and then go relieve Cecily."

"Yes, boss."

He turned back to her. "Let's go see what's up with Vern."

"Don't tell him I said he was in a snit." She quickened her step to keep up with him.

"Wasn't planning to. I'll say Marybeth asked me to sweet-talk him out of his chocolate cake recipe."

"He'll love hearing that. Is it true?"

He gave her a quick smile. "Yes, ma'am. Do you think I'd lie about a thing like that? I could get in trouble with Marybeth *and* Vern."

"But what a coincidence that she happened to ask for—"

"She just finished making a chocolate cake for tonight's birthday celebration, so it was on her mind. Sometimes things work out."

And sometimes they don't. But at least she'd made it through their first contact without falling apart. Mostly.

He held the swinging door open and she went in, clipped the new order to the metal carousel and picked up the orders waiting on the counter. Glancing through the window to make sure no one was coming, she backed out the door. She couldn't hear what Clint was saying to Vern, but the cook was grinning.

Five minutes into Clint's arrival and the tension was already seeping from her shoulders. If she'd ever doubted that he was essential to operating the Buffalo the way it should be done, that doubt had disappeared. Tough as their decision had been, they'd made the right one.

Thankfully the crowd emptied out in time to set up the dining room for dinner. Ironically, dinner would be easier on the wait staff because she and Clint had simplified the menu in anticipation of a big turnout. Next year they'd do the same with lunch.

While Cecily and Pam worked in the dining room, Tyra went over the door prize plans with Rance. He'd arrived dressed in an embroidered red vest over a pristine white shirt. A string tie completed the look of a riverboat gambler, clearly what he was going for.

She turned on the mic and coached Rance though some practice runs using her as the winning customer. Meanwhile Clint prepped the bar for what would be a busy night, but at least he and Rance would be in charge. He'd sent the frazzled young bartender home with a promise that he'd get some extra training before St. Patrick's Day.

By the time House Wine arrived and started tuning up, Tyra was satisfied that they were as ready as they could be. She sent Rance back over to the bar and ducked into the office to brush her hair and refresh her makeup.

She was using a compact mirror to put on a new coat of lipstick when someone rapped softly on the doorframe. Probably Cecily with a question. "Just a sec." Finishing, she glanced up and forgot to breathe.

Clint stood in the open doorway, concern clouding his blue eyes. "I didn't mean to startle you. I'm sorry."

"That's okay." She gulped in air and held tight to the lipstick tube. The business end was still rolled out. If she tried to retract it when she was shaking like this, she could end up with a streak of lipstick on her blouse. "Do you need...something?"

"Reassurance, I guess."

"About what?"

"That I'm not causing you problems."

"On the contrary. I was in a panic today. Everything settled down after you arrived."

"That makes me feel a little better. But when I first walked in this afternoon, you looked at me like...like I'd stabbed you. And just now, you had a deer-in-the-headlights expression, as if seeing me stressed you out. A lot."

Her brain turned to mush. What to say and how to say it? "We, um, kind of went from zero to sixty in a very short time."

"I suppose we did."

"And then we screeched to a stop."

His chest heaved. "Yes, ma'am. That's accurate."

"I haven't... I'm not... I need to get used to—"

"Me, too." He said it gently. "It'll take time."

"It will."

"But if it ever becomes too hard for you—" He glanced away and muttered something under his breath. "I mean, if it ever becomes too *tough* for you, I want you to—"

"I'll let you know." Would they ever be able to joke around the way they had before? Or was that over, too?

30

The next few hours passed in a blur for Tyra, but judging from the enthusiasm of the customers, the Valentine's party pleased everyone. The band was hot and Rance was in his element as the emcee doling out door prizes. Only a few diners weren't present to collect their gift certificate. Most stayed until the last winner was announced.

People left slowly, pausing to chat with others on their way out the door. This was what she had come home for, to live in a close community where folks knew their neighbors. She was so absorbed in watching the interaction that she almost missed Clint beckoning her over to the bar.

She walked toward him and leaned on the polished surface. "What's up?"

"Sky just texted. He wants to know if we're willing to have them all drive in for a small after-party at the Buffalo. They don't expect food, so we can close the kitchen and send Cecily and Pam home."

"It's okay with me if it's okay with you."

"I'm fine with it. They won't be here long, according to Sky. He's hoping the band will stay until they get here because Angie wants one dance to live music as part of her birthday celebration. Sky will hand them some extra cash if they're willing."

"I'll go ask them, but I'll bet they'll do it."

"Then I'll tell him to come on in. By the time they get here, they'll probably be the only ones in the place, which is how I think he wants it."

"Sounds like fun. I'll go check with the band." She went over and talked with Jim.

He answered with a smile. "Sure thing. We won't turn down a chance to earn a little extra. I remember that bunch from last Friday night. Will that guy Nick be with them?"

"No, he flew out last night."

"Too bad. He and that nice lady in the purple sure can dance. You and Clint came close that afternoon we auditioned but they've been at it longer. You two will get there someday."

She started to contradict him, then changed her mind. No point in getting into it. "We'll see."

"Let me know when they pull up outside. When they come in, we'll play the happy birthday song."

"Perfect." She thanked him for being flexible and went to help Cecily and Pam bus the rest of the tables. Those two were going out the back service door when several trucks pulled up in front. Tyra called out to Jim, and as the McLintock gang came through the door, the band launched into the birthday song.

They kept playing different versions as Angie danced her way through the tables followed by a noisy group of McLintocks. The Wenches were on hand, too, each dressed in her signature color. Colleen and Cindy had each brought their husbands, who'd been introduced to Tyra months ago as the Serving Boys. Everyone discarded coats, hats and scarves at the tables on their way to the dance floor.

The band finished up with a symbol crash and Angie leaped up on the bandstand to take a bow. Then she borrowed the mic from Jim. "For my birthday dance to live music, I want to dance with..." She surveyed the crowd. "All of you! So if the band can play *Boot Scootin' Boogie*—" She paused to glance at Jim, who gave her a thumbs up. "We'll get out there together and shake our booty, including Clint and Rance, so get over here, guys. You, too, Tyra. Marybeth and Buck, don't go sitting down. Nobody escapes."

Tyra couldn't help laughing as she stepped out on the floor. No one had more moxie than a newly minted twenty-five-year-old woman.

Angie moved through the crowd, tugging people from one line to another if she wasn't satisfied with the distribution. She insisted Clint stand next to Tyra. Obviously she hadn't received the memo that they weren't quite as friendly as they used to be.

Tyra glanced at Jess standing on her other side. "What did you do with the baby?"

"Molly's grammy offered to keep Maverick and Zach at her house until tomorrow morning. We accepted."

"Nice."

"We're all set, Mister Jim," Angie called out. "Hit it!"

The familiar music rocketed Tyra back to her teens line-dancing at the Buffalo with her girlfriends. She threw herself into it, determined not to falter, even when she spun around and was confronted with Clint's sexy ass moving in a way guaranteed to rev her engines.

The next time they were side by side, she looked over at him and he was looking back. Devil that he was, he flashed her a grin. She sent one back and added a shimmy. He missed a step but recovered fast enough not to cause a collision.

By the end of the dance she was breathless, and not only because of the dancing. The effect that man had on her should be illegal. She was trying to come up with something snappy to say to him when he leaned closer.

She shivered in anticipation.

"Okay if we give everyone one drink on the house?"

She blinked. Not a sweet nothing, after all. "Absolutely. I'll announce it so you can get ready to serve it." As he made tracks for the bar, she raised her voice. "Hey, everybody! In honor of Angie's birthday, everyone gets one free drink on the house. Band members included."

"Thanks, ma'am," Jim called out. "But we'll be packing up and heading out. This was fun. Happy birthday, Miss Angie."

"Thanks, Mister Jim!" She hurried over to the bar to claim her drink.

Eventually everyone was settled in a chair with a glass or a bottle in hand. Sky stood and raised his bottle of cider. "Here's to our little sis. Happy twenty-fifth, Angie!"

Shouting out *to Angie* along with everyone else, Tyra lifted her glass of ginger ale. In her present state, with no real idea of where she stood with the man behind the bar, she was better off not imbibing.

"Thanks, everybody. It's been a fabulous birthday. And as for what's about to happen next, this was my idea, although I had a lot of help from Kendall and Mom. If it turns into a mess — no wait, it's already a mess, so it can't get worse, right? Anyway, Clint, I need you to quit wiping down that bar and come over here with us."

"Okay." He sounded wary, but he did it. "Any certain spot?"

"Yes. Next to Tyra."

He hesitated. "Hey, Angie. I know it's your birthday, but—"

"Yes, it is, at least for another—" She glanced at the antique wall clock. "Thirty-seven minutes. This won't take that long. Please sit down."

Tyra looked over at him as he settled into the chair positioned right next to hers. Someone had put it there, probably his sister.

He gave her a shrug before turning his attention back to the birthday girl.

She pulled some notes out of her pocket, glanced at them and shoved them back inside. "I'm going to be the voice of the Buffalo."

"*What?*" Tyra and Clint shouted in unison. Then they shared a look of pure panic.

"Settle down. I don't mean the voice of the wooden buffalo. I could never pull that off."

Tyra let out a sigh. Clint echoed it.

"Pretend I'm the voice of this building we all love so much, that the town loves so much. But I'm just a building with no say-so about what happens to me. I depend on the people who have the say-so, Clint and Tyra. It's like they're the parents and I'm their kid. Adopted kid, since they didn't give birth to me."

Tyra exchanged a *what-the-hell?* glance with Clint.

"Hey, guys, it's a metaphor. Just go with it." Angie took a breath and continued. "Clint and Tyra love me to pieces. They also get along great. Despite that, they've decided that I'll be better off if they keep their distance from each other and have joint custody of me. I don't get it. They'll take much better care of me if they stay together because they'll both be happier."

Tyra sat in stunned silence, not looking at Clint except from the corner of her eye. He sat silent and unmoving, too.

Beau left his chair and came over to put his arm around Angie. "Great job. I'm not sure they got it, but give them time. It might sink in."

"Oh, I get it." Clint straightened and glanced up. "But Tyra and I have talked this through and we've decided it's too risky to have a romantic relationship that might go sour. It wasn't easy for us to come to that conclusion, but we firmly believe it's in the best interests of the Buffalo."

Beau let out a frustrated sigh. "Are you even listening to yourself? You and Tyra came to this conclusion *together*. According to my intel, you're in *complete agreement*. You're denying your feelings for each other, making this huge sacrifice for the good of the Buffalo! If you can cooperate to that degree, how can you possibly imagine a day when you won't get along? Or that you'd ever let any disagreement harm the Buffalo? Where's the risk? Holy shit, this is a match made in heaven!"

"He's right." Cheyenne put down his drink. "You guys have been in tune ever since Tyra came on board. We've all watched it for two years and you haven't had a major blowup yet. Why would that change? If you're great business partners, why couldn't you be great partners, period?"

Desiree stood. "You won't be surprised to hear that I agree with what's been said. In fact, everyone in this room agrees, including the Wenches, and we hardly ever agree completely on anything. But we've said our piece, so we'll take off and leave you to discuss it. Or not. Clint, I'd like to see you privately for a minute."

He stood. "In the office?"

"No, just over in that corner." She walked to the back of the dining room.

Tyra got up, along with everyone else. Angie gave her the first hug, followed by everyone else. Kendall was last.

Folding her close, she murmured in her ear. "Tell him you love him. He doesn't know and he needs to know."

"But—"

Kendall pulled back and looked her in the eye. "Tell him. Take that risk, girlfriend." After another quick hug, Kendall left to join the others walking out the door, each of them setting off the buffalo's drawling *Byyyye, byyyyye, Valentiiiiine.*

Tyra glanced across the room where Clint was in deep conversation with his mother. Then he gave her a tight hug.

The sweet moment made Tyra's chest swell and her throat tighten. She was so warm inside. Tears filled her eyes but she wasn't sad. Instead she was...in love?

31

Clint mulled over his mom's words as she walked away.

She passed by the buffalo, triggering its farewell message, which made her laugh. "I love that voice. Reminds me of someone but I can't think of who it is. See you two kids later."

"Bye, Mom." He waited until she was out the door. Then he crossed the room, stopping a few feet away from Tyra. "That was unexpected."

"Sure was."

Struggling to order his thoughts, he massaged the back of his neck. "I hate to admit it, because it makes me feel like an idiot, but they might have a point."

"They might." She was quiet, her emerald gaze totally focused on him.

What was she thinking? Probably turning the events over in her mind, just like he was. He kept talking, trying to make sense of it all. "I mean, we do get along pretty well." He paused. "Or we did, until Saturday night."

Her breath caught. "Uh-huh."

"That wasn't much fun."

"No."

"Well, I mean it was fun...until it wasn't."

"Mm."

"I guess it boils down to me thinking you're off limits because you're the boss and you've had the idea that I'm off-limits because I work for you, but it's not like you treat me like an underling. I've never let the boss-employee situation stop me from saying what's on my mind." At least when it came to the Buffalo. "It's possible we've blown the whole thing out of propor—"

"I love you."

A jolt of adrenaline shot through him, leaving him shaking like a newborn foal. "W-what?"

"I *love* you." She sounded bewildered by the concept and her eyes glistened with tears. "Kendall said that I did on Sunday but I didn't—"

"Hey, you've been through a lot." *Don't take her seriously, dude. That could be suicide.* His heart pounded so loud that his ears buzzed. "It's been a long day. I'm sure you're exhausted. I think—"

"But it's true." She stepped closer. "Whenever I look at you, I get this squeeze in my chest, and the urge to hug you." She swiped at her eyes. "And not just because you're sexy and you turn me on, which you are and you do, but because I want to be close to you, to feel your arms around me, to see you smile, to hear you laugh." She sniffed. "I love you, Clint. And my nose is dripping, and I don't have a—"

"Here." He whipped a bandana out of his back pocket and handed it to her. Then he pulled her into his arms. To comfort her. That was all he'd do. She'd been wound tight since the moment he'd walked in this afternoon. Then his family, his loving, buttinsky family, had sent her over the edge. "I won't apologize for my family because they only want the best for both of us, but—"

"But they're right!" She wiped her nose and balled up the bandana. "Beau's right. We're a match made in freaking heaven!"

"You just think so because he's a very convincing—"

"I don't *think*. I *know*." She looked up at him. "It's so easy to see it now. I've been in love with you for months, but I refused to put a name to it."

He swallowed. Oh, he wanted to believe her. But after so long….

"I kept focusing on the advice in my business management books. *Keep romance out of the office.* But this isn't an office." Her voice wobbled and she sniffed again. "It's our baby."

His throat hurt. "In a way."

"But you still don't believe that I love you." Dropping his bandana on the floor, she reached up and cupped his face in both hands. "Maybe this will help." Rising to her toes, she kissed him.

The tender, warm touch of her lips tore at his heart. Could it possibly be true? Did he dare believe her?

Then she drew back. "Tell me that didn't affect you."

"It did." The words came out sounding gruff. He cleared his throat. "But that's—"

"You love me, too. I can feel it in your kiss. But it would be nice to hear you say it."

His mom's words came back. *Tell her. She needs to know.* He took a ragged breath. "I've loved you since I was fourteen. I've never stopped." The glow in her eyes brightened, so he went for broke. "I love you even more now."

"L-lucky me." Tears dampened her cheeks as her gaze searched his. "So, given that I love you and you love me... do you..." She gulped. "Do you have plans for—"

"The rest of my life?" His world shifted, trembled. Tim and Faith's song. She wouldn't reference it unless...unless *she loved him*. The dam burst and he could barely speak as emotions crowded his chest and clogged his throat. Finally he managed to choke out the words. "I do...if you'll marry me."

"I will." And she kissed him again, leaving absolutely no doubt that she loved him with a passion that made him breathless and dizzy with joy.

Seventeen years of waiting and hoping. He came up for air, pulled her close again and kissed her with all the love in his heart. Seventeen long years. Worth every second. For this.

*****

Cowgirl Angelique McLintock's romantic
aspirations get cut off at the pass by her posse
of overprotective big brothers in TEMPTING
THE COWBOY'S SISTER, book six in the Rowdy
Ranch series!

*****

New York Times bestselling author Vicki Lewis Thompson's love affair with cowboys started with the Lone Ranger, continued through Maverick, and took a turn south of the border with Zorro. She views cowboys as the Western version of knights in shining armor, rugged men who value honor, honesty and hard work. Fortunately for her, she lives in the Arizona desert, where broad-shouldered, lean-hipped cowboys abound. Blessed with such an abundance of inspiration, she only hopes that she can do them justice.

For more information about this prolific author, visit her website and sign up for her newsletter. She loves connecting with readers.

VickiLewisThompson.com

Printed in the USA
CPSIA information can be obtained
at www.ICGtesting.com
CBHW031158130824
13123CB00008B/174